Slowly an idea began to bloom in my mind. What if I was somehow able to get my mom to agree to take in Lily? Of course, fostering an older dog like Lily wouldn't be her first choice. But if I got her to give it a try, my mom could see how wonderful all dogs were, not just dogs with tons of training. Lily was so special—my mom had to see that. If she loved Lily half as much as I did, maybe we'd even get to adopt her. And that would be bliss!

Roxbury Park • Dog Club

Roxbury Park DOg Club

A NEW LEASH ON LIFE

DAPHNE MAPLE

HARPER

An Imprint of HarperCollinsPublishers

Roxbury Park Dog Club #5: A New Leash on Life

Text by Daphne Maple, copyright © 2017 by HarperCollins Publishers

Illustrations © 2017 by Annabelle Metayer

www.harpercollinschildrens.com

Library of Congress Control Number: 2016938992

ISBN 978-0-06-237100-3 (pbk.)

Typography by Jenna Stempel

16 17 18 19 20   OPM   10 9 8 7 6 5 4 3 2 1

First Edition

For Chloe Grace

1

"Hey, Bri," Taylor said to me somewhat breathlessly as she came into our locker alcove. Elbowing through the crowd at the end of the day at Roxbury Park Middle School could leave a girl winded like that.

"Hey," I replied, happy to see her. Which was a big change: Not so long ago Taylor had been my number one enemy. I'd been jealous of how easy it was for her to be the new girl at the start of the year, becoming best friends with Kim and Sasha, two of the nicest girls in seventh grade, and helping them start their Dog Club. I'd been new the year before and still felt like an outsider, so seeing Taylor fit in that smoothly made me mad. Some people keep their angry and jealous feelings to themselves, but not me. I spoke up, especially when I was upset, and sometimes I didn't think before I started talking. That wasn't a good idea because some pretty mean things came out. Taylor saw through all that, though, which is just one example of how awesome she is. And ever since, I've really been working on thinking before opening my mouth. I don't want to be the mean girl ever again.

"You ready?" Taylor asked. She was stuffing books into her backpack.

"Yeah," I said, brushing back a stray wisp of my long black hair. I liked playing around with creative hairstyles and today I had a sock bun that I'd rolled up carefully this morning. It sat like a shiny fat doughnut on top of my head, making me look tall.

"Let's go," Taylor said with an easy grin, leading the way out of the alcove. She had to maneuver around kids hanging out talking as they packed up for the day. Before, I'd linger too, but now I had a place to go, and I was eager to get there. Taylor was too. Who wouldn't be excited about two and a half hours of play with the cutest dogs in all of Roxbury Park?

We just had one more stop to go before we'd be on our way.

"I hope Kim did well on that math test," Taylor said. The beads in her braids swung around her face as she spoke. The day before she'd gotten new ones, a mix of lavender and turquoise that looked great with her dark brown skin and big brown eyes.

"Yeah, me too," I said. Our friend Kim was a genius when it came to dogs—the Dog Club was her idea and everyone called her the dog whisperer because of the way she understood and trained pups of all shapes and sizes. But math and English tripped her up, and we'd had a scare when it looked like her parents wanted her to change schools to improve her grades. However, with the help of Taylor and Sasha, Kim had set up tutoring sessions with Taylor's sister Anna, and all of us quizzed her before exams. So far it was working great and when we rounded the corner, I could see her grinning as she chatted with Sasha in front of her locker.

"Kim aced the test," Sasha told us gleefully as we came up to them.

"Awesome," Taylor said, raising her hand to high-five Kim.

"Yeah, that's great," I echoed, not sure if I should high-five too. I knew that Kim and Sasha accepted me as part of their group; after all, they asked me to join the Dog Club and that showed how much they trusted me, which was great. But I had to admit there were still moments when I felt a little like a fourth wheel when the four of us were together. You'd think a fourth wheel would even everything out, but the three of them had inside jokes and memories all their own. And there was an easiness between them that sometimes felt like an invisible barrier, with them on the inside and me on the outside. Still, I was thrilled to be part of the gang and excited for our afternoon at the club. And I hoped that at some point that barrier would come down and I'd be fully on the inside too.

"Thanks, guys," Kim said, her brown eyes bright as she smiled. "I couldn't have done it without your help. And of course Anna's."

Anna was one of Taylor's three older sisters and a math genius. She and Taylor hadn't always gotten along, but lately they were close as could be and Anna had really come through to help Kim.

"Anna's the best," Taylor said proudly. "Are you guys ready to go? The dogs are waiting."

"Then let's get moving," Sasha said cheerfully. Her brown curls were pulled back in a braid and she moved gracefully, probably because she was a star dancer at the school where she studied ballet, tap, and jazz. "Bri, is it your day to get Mr. S? Because I need to give you the key to our house. I had to use the spare yesterday and I forgot to put it back in the hiding place under the plant box."

Sasha was kind of scatterbrained, but she was so good natured about it that it didn't matter. And her cheeks glowed a healthy pink every time she talked about her dog, Mr. S. Not so long ago he'd lived at the Roxbury Park Dog Shelter, where Kim, Sasha, and Taylor had started the Dog Club, both to help owners who worked all day get exercise and attention for their pets, and to raise money for the shelter. But Sasha had fallen in love with him and managed to talk her neat-freak mom into adopting him. Now he had a home with Sasha and came with us to the club to see all his old pals a few times a week.

"Yes, I'm getting Mr. S, Humphrey, and Popsicle," I confirmed. One of the perks we offered Dog Club customers was pickup service. For owners with full-time jobs, the club was the perfect way for their dogs to get a good workout and lots of love and doggy company while they were at work. And for a small additional fee we'd get their dogs on our way to the shelter.

Sasha handed me her key and I put it in my pocket. We wove through the crowd and finally made it out into the brisk fall afternoon. There was a chilly wind, but the sun was warm on my face as we headed into town, our feet crunching on recently fallen leaves. Autumn had definitely come to Roxbury Park.

"I'm getting Coco and Waffles," Taylor said, "since I got Gus and Hattie the last time." Waffles was a shelter dog recently adopted by the Datta family, who had immediately signed him up for the club. Waffles clearly loved his new home but was always happy to see his old friends at the shelter.

"Sounds good," Sasha agreed. We tried to rotate pickups with the exception of one dog.

"How's Missy doing with the walk to the shelter?" I asked Kim. Missy was a new club dog and she actually belonged to our English teacher, Mrs. Benson, who was the strictest teacher any of us had ever had. We were shocked when she showed up at the shelter in jeans and a T-shirt like a regular person, needing help with her new dog. Missy had been rescued from a puppy mill where she had been badly mistreated. She had been like a shadow, scared of everything and cringing whenever anyone got too close. But Kim the dog whisperer had worked her magic, while Mrs. Benson had patiently showered Missy with love, and the little Yorkie was finally coming out of her shell.

"She's doing great," Kim said with a grin. "She loves all the smells on Main Street."

"Like Sugar and Spice?" Taylor asked. Sugar and Spice was the candy store in town and it smelled like chocolate, cinnamon, and strawberries every time we passed. It made my mouth water just to think about it.

"Actually Missy really likes the garbage can on the corner in front of the bank," Kim said, laughing. "She's into two-day-old sandwiches and crusty bits of dough-nut."

"Gross," Taylor said, making a sour face that cracked all of us up.

"You should see Mr. S dig into his Buddy's Beef Stew," Sasha said, wrinkling her nose. "Just opening the can kills my appetite for hours, but he acts like it's the tastiest meal ever."

"What does your mom feed the dogs at the Pampered Puppy?" Taylor asked me. "Do they get gourmet dog food?"

Her tone was light, but I felt my stomach tighten at her words. "Um, yeah," I said. "But it still smells pretty gross." The organic fresh minced meat used at the Pampered Puppy actually smelled fine, but I didn't want to make a big deal about it. My mom ran a dog spa that was pretty much a fancy version of our Dog Club. But where our dogs just played and had fun, the dogs who came to the Pampered Puppy got training and each one had an individualized exercise program, as well as regular grooming sessions and carefully planned diets. It was great for people who wanted their dogs obedient and spotless at the end of the day. But I was a lot more comfortable at our Dog Club, where owners just laughed if their dogs were revved up and a bit on the muddy side at pickup.

"Is the new dog coming to Dog Club today?" I asked, wanting to change the subject.

"Yes," Sasha confirmed. She handled all the clients who came to the club, while Kim wrote entries in our blog, the Dog Club Diaries. Taylor took photos for the blog, and recently for a newspaper story that had gotten us more clients than we could handle. We now had a waiting list and one lucky dog had just gotten off it. "Her name is Jinx and she's coming in for her visit today. Her owners say she's mischievous—hopefully she's not another Sierra."

The three of them laughed and I tried to join in. Sierra was a dog who'd been too wild for the club and caused all kinds of problems. I wasn't part of the club then, though, so it was one of those fourth-wheel moments. At least I knew about the visits. Now when a dog wanted to join the club they had an initial visit, to see how they got along with the other dogs and if they were a good fit for the loose, easygoing culture of our Dog Club.

We'd reached the corner where we separated to get our dogs.

"See you guys in a little bit," Sasha called as she and Kim headed straight, while Taylor turned left and I turned right down Spring Street. Sasha and Kim lived a block and a half down, and the Cronins, who had been the first Dog Club members, were right next to Kim's house. I headed to their house and as soon as I slipped the key into the lock of the front door and opened it, I heard a dog let out a happy bark.

"Hi, Popsicle," I said warmly, bending down to pet the black and white puppy with floppy ears. The Cronins had adopted Popsicle from the shelter and like all the dogs she loved her time in Dog Club with her pals.

"And hello to you too, Humphrey," I said to the basset hound making his way slowly into the front hall. Humphrey was a typical basset and didn't rush for anything except food. When he reached us he fell over onto one side, breathing heavily, as though the walk from the living room had exhausted him.

"You are one lazy pup," I told him affectionately, not meaning a word of it. I stroked his silky ears and he let out a contented sigh.

After a little more snuggling, I grabbed their leashes and buckled them on, and we headed over to get Mr. S. When I first met Mr. S I was confused by the way he sometimes ran into things. I was actually a little rude about it after he banged into my elbow, but Sasha, protective doggy mom, set me straight fast. Mr. S, a fluffy white Cavachon, was nearly blind. And considering that, it was amazing how well he got by. Now I loved him almost as much as Sasha did, and seeing him race about in happy circles when the dogs and I arrived to get him made me smile. I bent down and hugged him. Mr. S rewarded me with a kiss and then rushed to romp with his friends.

"Okay, guys, let's get this show on the road," I told my pack of three. Sasha was supposed to leave Mr. S's leash on a hook by the door, but as usual it wasn't there. It took me a minute, but I soon found it thrown over the hall chair, where Sasha had probably tossed it after walking Mr. S this morning. Mr. S stood still while I snapped the leash onto his collar and a minute later we were on our way.

2

It was fun walking down Main Street with three happy dogs that half the town seemed to know. Before Roxbury Park my family had lived in Washington, DC. I still missed the Chinatown there and all the great restaurants. My family was Chinese American, and we could be picky about the best cooked dishes. But aside from that, I was very happy to be in Roxbury Park.

"Hi, Brianna," Kim's dad said. He was just walking

into the Rox, the diner Kim's family owned. "On your way to Dog Club?"

"Yeah," I said, a little shyly. Mr. Feeney was super nice, but it was always weird to see your friend's parents when your friend wasn't there.

"Have fun," he said with a wave.

I stopped to admire the new window display at Sugar and Spice, the candy store. The older couple who had originally owned it had recently retired and moved to New Mexico. None of us had met the new owners yet, but their window displays were awesome. This one was a candy version of Roxbury Park, with chocolate buildings, lollipop trees, marzipan people, and little cars made out of gumdrops. It looked good enough to eat, which of course was the idea.

"Have a good Dog Club meeting, Bri," said Anya Skakov, who worked at the Ice Creamery. She was heading into Sugar and Spice, probably to pick up candy toppings for the sundaes and mix-ins that made the Ice Creamery so delicious.

"Thanks," I said, loving that she knew me and knew exactly where I was going. This was one of the many things that made Roxbury Park such a wonderful place to live.

The second I walked into the shelter, a medium-size tan dog with shaggy fur and a big doggy smile ran up as though she'd been waiting for me.

"Hi, Lily!" I exclaimed, wrapping my arms around her as soon as I'd freed my mini dog pack from their leashes. I loved all the dogs in the shelter, as well as all our club members, but Lily was special. She was sweet and playful and sensitive too. She knew just when you needed a few extra doggy kisses. And lately it seemed like she was always near me, keeping an eye on what I was doing and coming up to me more often than anyone else. I loved nothing more than snuggling her. At home, when my dad was away on business and it was just me and my mom, I sometimes thought how great it would be to have Lily in my room, cuddled up next to me while I did homework and texted my friends.

A moment later, Boxer, who was a boxer, of course, bounded up with his favorite green Frisbee in his mouth. There was a time when I thought the chewed-up toy, which was always slimy with dog drool, was kind of gross. But that was before I realized how much Boxer loved it. And today I didn't hesitate to take it when he dropped it at my feet and give it a hearty toss across the room. Boxer and Lily bounded after it and Popsicle and Mr. S dashed after them. Humphrey walked more slowly as he made his way over to the corner where Missy was standing. Lately Missy and Humphrey had been bonding, probably because Humphrey was so mellow. Missy would likely always have some issues from her time at the puppy mill, but watching her sniff Humphrey in greeting, and then trot after him when Kim threw a tennis ball, melted my heart.

"Those two are so cute," I said, walking over to Kim.

"Tell me about it," Kim said with a grin. Sasha had already arrived with Gus, a sweet brown lab, and Hattie, a shy sheepdog puppy and another former shelter dog who came back for Dog Club. The two of them were playing fetch with Sasha and Tuesday, a new shelter dog who had short black curly fur and a curlicue tail. Daisy, a feisty brown dachshund whose owner dropped her off for Dog Club, was last to arrive but immediately joined Tuesday and Sasha.

The main room of the shelter was big and open, with a new linoleum floor. There was a small bathroom off to one side, as well as the room where dog food was stored, though the dogs were usually fed after we left. Alice's office was up front, while bins of toys were stored on the shelves along one side wall. The other side wall was lined with cages that each had a soft doggy bed and blanket. That was where the dogs slept at night, but they were always open during the day, in case a dog wanted to take a nap or spend a little quiet time alone. Out back was a big fenced-in yard where we often took the dogs to play on warm days.

I was about to throw the Frisbee again when the

front door opened and Coco, Waffles, and Taylor came in, followed by Tim and Caley, the two high school volunteers.

"Hey, gang," Tim said, running a hand through his black hair and making it stick up all over the place. "Doggy basketball in five. Bri, this time you're going down."

I laughed at that. Doggy basketball was a game Tim invented that involved a big orange ball and a laundry basket. We'd divide the dogs into teams and coach them to get baskets and for some reason I was unbeaten. If doggy basketball were a real sport I could probably lead an Olympic team to gold. But as it was, Tim was endlessly trying to come up with ways to beat me.

"You're on," I said. "I'll even give you first pick."

Tim narrowed his eyes. "Nice try, but I can tell you're using mind tricks to defeat me. You get first pick."

Caley rolled her eyes. "Someone's getting a little paranoid," she said, grinning at me.

"It wasn't a mind trick at all," I said, opening my eyes wide to look innocent. "Or was it?" I added in an evil, hushed voice.

Caley burst out laughing as Tim pointed at me. "See? She's like an evil Sith lord."

"A what?" Caley asked.

Now it was Tim rolling his eyes. "Caley, you're a cultural illiterate because you've never seen *Star Wars*. You have to do something about this."

It was not the first time they'd had this squabble and the four of us exchanged amused glances. It was nice to be on the inside of the joke.

"Hey, everybody," Alice said, walking out of her office and plucking some dog fur off her T-shirt that had different color dog prints running across it. Alice was the owner of the shelter and a pretty amazing dog whisperer in her own right. Her long hair was falling out of its usual ponytail and her face was free of makeup. Her job was the same as my mom's: running a dog-care center. But they couldn't have been more different. My mom never had a hair out of place, her makeup was always perfect, and she wore a pristine, fitted lab coat with the words "Pampered Puppy" embroidered on it. She was every inch the sleek, professional business-woman, while Alice was more the comfortable, relaxed dog lover who just happened to run a business. But I shook my head to clear away the thought. I preferred not to think about my mom or the Pampered Puppy when I was at the shelter.

"I have a new project I'm working on," Alice announced. Boxer ran up and threw himself down at Alice's feet. She knelt to give him a good belly scratch and continued. "All the publicity we've gotten in the past few weeks has led to some organizations reaching out to us to see if we have room to take in new dogs, especially shelters that haven't adopted a no-kill policy."

"You mean shelters that put down the animals if they are there too long," Kim said darkly.

Alice sighed and her eyes were sad. "There are so many stray animals that shelters get full," she said. "Like we are here. And so some shelters choose to put down animals that haven't been adopted."

"It's awful," I said, crossing my arms over my chest. The thought of innocent animals being killed because they couldn't find a home made me both furious and sad. Lily, sensing my distress, came over and looked up at me with her sweet brown eyes. I sat on the floor and hugged her close.

"It's a hard situation," Alice said. "But I agree with you, Bri. Killing animals is not the answer. Finding them homes is. Which is why I want to start a fostering program."

I liked the idea of a solution that saved pets, but I wasn't sure what fostering was. And I could tell by the way Taylor was frowning and Sasha was pulling on a stray curl that I wasn't alone.

"That's when people take in animals on a short-term basis, while permanent homes are found for them, right?" Kim asked. Missy and Humphrey had settled down on either side of her and she was petting them both.

Alice nodded. I wasn't surprised that Kim knew this because she seemed to know everything when it came to dogs.

"That's right," Alice said. "I'm hoping we can find people willing to host dogs for a month or two. We'll ramp up our advertising, both to find foster families and to find people who will ultimately adopt the dogs."

"Can foster families adopt the dogs they take in?" Tim asked. He was throwing a ball for Hattie, Daisy, Popsicle, Tuesday, and Mr. S, but was still following the conversation.

"Yes, absolutely," Alice said. "One of the great things about a fostering program is that families who are considering getting a pet can try it out for a month or two and see how it works for them. Often they fall in love with the animal they've taken in and start the process to adopt."

"That sounds like a happy ending," Sasha said. Gracie dropped a blue plastic bone at her feet and Sasha gave it a toss across the big room. Gracie, Waffles, and Gus raced after it.

"Yes, exactly," Alice said. "That's what I'm hoping for, a bunch of happy endings. The shelters that have contacted me are hoping for that too. So the sooner we start finding foster homes for the dogs who need them, the better."

"What can we do to help?" I asked. Lily was still nestled in next to me and I rubbed her head with my knuckles.

Alice grinned at me, which made me happy I'd asked. "We're going to design flyers and then put them up everywhere," she said. "And I was hoping you'd be willing to ask your mom to put one up at the Pampered Puppy. I know there are a lot of dog lovers there and I bet some would be willing to help a dog in need."

My body tensed up at the request and Lily, feeling the change, burrowed in even closer to me. "Um, sure," I said, hearing how fake my voice sounded. Luckily no one seemed to notice.

"I'll put one up at the Rox," Kim said.

"And I know my mom will put some up at her law

firm," Sasha said, while Taylor nodded. Sasha's mom was an environmental lawyer and Taylor's dad worked with her. They were old law school friends and enjoyed trying cases together. Their office would be a good place to post notices about the fostering program since they had a lot of clients.

"I'll help put them around town," I said, relieved to have the focus off the Pampered Puppy. "We all will."

"Definitely," Taylor agreed, while Kim and Sasha nodded.

"We'll post a bunch at the high school," Caley said. "And I'll see if we can pass them out with the programs for the fall musical."

"Oh, great idea," Alice said. "I'm glad everyone can help, not that I'm surprised." She smiled, though it was tinged with sadness. "I know we all want to do everything we can to help save these dogs."

We all nodded.

"Now we just have to design the flyers," Alice said.

"Bri can help with that," Taylor said immediately.

"She's great at art and graphic design."

Her words made me feel warm all over. It was true that I really liked drawing and using the computer to design things.

"Bri, I didn't know that," Kim said.

"You should make us a logo for the flyers," Taylor said, grinning at me.

"I'd love to do that," I said, twisting my hands shyly. "I can start working on it tonight."

"That would be wonderful," Alice said. "The sooner we have flyers ready, the better."

"Perfect," Taylor said, giving me a thumbs-up.

I smiled at her gratefully. Taylor really had my back. I didn't even remember telling her about my interest in art, since it was mostly something I did by myself at home. But here she was, giving me the chance to use it for the club. She really was the best.

Just then the door opened and a small reddish-tan furry head with pointed ears and a fox face poked in, followed by a slightly frazzled-looking young woman.

"Stay, Jinx," she said to the little fox dog.

But Jinx had spotted the toys, the dogs, and the wide open space, and was ready to go. Her nails scraped on the floor as she tried to escape her leash and join in the fun.

"Hi, I'm Alice, and this is Kim, Sasha, Taylor, and Bri, the Roxbury Park Dog Club members," Alice said with a smile. "And our high school volunteers Tim and Caley. Welcome."

"Thanks, and great to meet all of you," the woman said. "Sasha, I'm Violet; we spoke a few times."

"Right," Sasha said, all business. "We're happy to have Jinx here for her first visit to the club."

"I think she's eager to get started," Violet said with a sheepish grin as Jinx tried to make another break for it.

Kim bent down and held out her hand for Jinx to sniff. Then she began to pet Jinx, rubbing gently behind her furry ears. "Sit," Kim said kindly but firmly, and Jinx sat.

"Kim is our dog whisperer," Sasha said.

Violet looked impressed. "She really is," she said. "It normally takes me three tries and a doggy treat to get Jinx to do anything I say."

"I can give you some pointers if you want," Kim offered.

"I'd love that," Violet said. "Jinx is a real sweetie, but getting her to come to me in the dog park can be a true exercise in patience."

We all laughed at that.

"You can let her off the leash whenever you're ready," Kim said.

Violet released Jinx, who took a moment to see what looked like the best game, then ran over to join Tim, Boxer, Hattie, and Coco playing fetch with Boxer's Frisbee. The other dogs took a moment to sniff Jinx, who sniffed back good-naturedly. Then Tim tossed the Frisbee and the playing began.

"She fits right in," Violet said happily.

It really was easy for dogs to make new friends. You could tell Jinx wasn't feeling like a fourth wheel at all.

"She does," Taylor agreed, taking out her camera and snapping some pictures. "We put photos on our blog after every meeting. Is it okay if I put up some of Jinx?"

"That'd be great," Violet said. "I'd love to see her in action."

"We post in the Dog Club Diary after every meeting too," Sasha said. Kim was in charge of that. "So you know exactly what Jinx does when she's with us."

"Great," Violet said, smiling. "She's my baby and I'm relieved to know she'll be having fun while I'm at work."

"We can pretty much guarantee she'll enjoy herself," Taylor said as Jinx raced past looking utterly blissful.

"You can leave her with us for the rest of the afternoon," Sasha said, sounding professional. "And as long as it all goes well, she can become a regular member of the club. Let me tell you about our pickup service and also our new fostering program in case you know anyone who might be interested."

Sasha was going to be a great businesswoman when she grew up. I never would have thought to mention the fostering, but it was a great idea. The more people who learned about our new program the better.

Sasha led Violet toward Alice's office.

"Who wants to go outside?" Kim asked.

"Good idea," Caley said, looking around at the groups of dogs frisking around the room.

"I'll go," I said.

"Not so fast, Bri," Tim said, hands on his hips. "Or are you scared that this is the day I upset your record in doggy basketball?"

"No way," I said, laughing. "Let's play some doggy basketball."

3

I was tired when I got home that night, but my coaching record in doggy basketball remained unbroken. That and all the fun with the dogs had me in a good mood when I walked into the dark house. I usually got home before my mom and it was my job to start dinner. When my dad was around he got home even later, but he was generally gone two weeks of every month on trips for work. Though now he was away for even longer: three whole weeks traveling between Singapore, China, and Japan. He always brought me back great presents, and when he went to China he came home with spices we used for the stir-fries and clay pot casseroles my mom made. But that didn't make up for how much I missed him when he was away. He tried to video chat with us at night, even if he had to get up early to do it, but it wasn't the same as having him here.

The house was cold so after I switched on the lights I turned up the heat. Not surprisingly the living room and connected dining room were spotless. My mom liked everything neat at all times. But our house was homey too, with a squashy green sofa and two plush armchairs in the living room, Chinese scrolls depicting flowers and mountains on the walls, and a thick rug that kept my feet toasty even in winter, since we never wore shoes inside.

I headed past the big oak table that could seat eight but usually just sat me and my mom, and into the kitchen that was, of course, gleaming. My mom loved to cook, but she cleaned as she went so there were never piles of dishes on the counter.

I checked the whiteboard on the fridge where my mom wrote out the dinner schedule and saw that tonight was sautéed eggplant and fried pork over rice. I got the rice started in the cooker and was just pulling the eggplant out of the fridge when my mom came in.

I heard her hang up her coat, put her shoes away, and put on the slippers that she wore around the house. Then she padded into the kitchen. I was short, but my mom was what my dad called petite, so I was nearly as tall as she was, which was kind of cool.

"Hi, Bun," she said, planting a kiss on my cheek. Bun was her nickname for me, short for our favorite dessert, steamed sweet bean paste buns. "How was your day?"

"Good," I said, getting out a cutting board. "I think I did well on my English quiz. There was a trick question about the conch, but I'm pretty sure I got it right." We'd just started reading *Lord of the Flies* in Mrs.

Benson's class and so far it was really good.

"Nice work," my mom said. She was slicing up the pork. "It's satisfying to be prepared and then do well, isn't it?"

"Yes," I said, trying not to sigh. Being prepared was one of my mom's favorite things to lecture about.

"I loved that book when I was young," my mom went on. "It makes you think a lot about human nature."

"That's what Mrs. Benson said too," I agreed. I was peeling the eggplant, the skin coming off in long, thin strips.

"Maybe I missed my calling as an English teacher," my mom said with a smile.

"You'd run a tight ship, just like Mrs. Benson," I said.

"Yes," my mom said, like this was a compliment. Which it kind of was, since Mrs. Benson's class was actually my favorite.

"Rules are important," my mom went on. "People need routine and structure to succeed. Dogs too."

Uh-oh. This was exactly what I didn't want to talk about. But once my mom got on this topic, it was pretty much impossible to stop her.

"Dogs are happiest when they get training and proper stimulation," my mom went on. She'd prepared a plate of flour with spices and was rolling the pork strips in the mixture, then setting them in the sizzling wok. She had to talk a bit louder to be heard over the sound, but my mom had a voice that carried.

"Right," I said. "What time is dad calling?" It was worth a try to see if I could derail her.

"Seven thirty," my mom said. "And that's why I don't understand why you prefer to work at the shelter instead of our dog spa." There was no derailing. And she said the word *shelter* like she was saying *garbage dump*.

"It's fun and my friends are there," I said. It wasn't the first time I'd tried to explain.

"But the dogs just run around, helter-skelter," my mom said. She sounded genuinely puzzled. "And the facility is falling apart."

"Mom, you've never even been there," I chided her.

"Yes, but I've seen pictures," my mom said. "The floor is all scratched up, the toys are strewn about. It's scruffy and unkempt."

"It's cozy and comfortable," I countered. "We have a great time with the dogs and they have a great time with us."

"Yes, but they don't get trained or groomed," my mom said. "Their individual needs aren't taken into account."

"Their need to play is taken into account," I said. The eggplant was chopped up into neat cubes, just how my mom liked it. I slid the plate over to her and after she'd taken the pork out of the wok, she put in more sesame oil, then the eggplant, which she covered with minced garlic, ginger, and soy sauce.

"Dogs have more needs than that," my mother said dismissively as she stirred. "Skills they need to learn and ways they should be challenged. That's why we evaluate every dog we accept at the Pampered Puppy and create a plan just for that animal."

"I know," I said, trying not to be impatient. But we'd had this conversation a thousand times and it was starting to wear on me. Plus I was starving.

"It's better for the dogs," my mom said primly, like that was just a given fact instead of her opinion.

Dinner was ready so I got a break as we brought the food into the dining room, along with bowls and chopsticks. But as soon as my mom had served us each a mound of steaming rice, she started in again. "I just don't understand why you want to waste your time in a second-rate care center like the shelter instead of working with me at the Pampered Puppy," she said bluntly.

"It's not second-rate," I snapped. Then I took a bite of food so I wouldn't completely lose my temper.

"But Bun, it is," my mother said. "It's an unstructured free-for-all that would probably fail a board inspection."

"The shelter would pass any inspection because it's clean and the dogs are well cared for," I said, scooping up more pork. The sooner I was done, the sooner I could go up to my room and end this conversation.

"That setup is an accident waiting to happen," my mom said firmly. "Plus look at the dogs you take in and how they're handled. There's no training at all. And then there are those older dogs who are nearly impossible to teach after years of bad habits. That's most of the problem right there."

I thought of sweet Lily, the way she followed me around, came to me when I was upset, and seemed to know how I was feeling much better than my mother did right now. "I love the dogs at the shelter," I said, suddenly feeling almost tearful. Which was how these conversations always went: my mom pushed until she upset me. Before, I'd get angry and say something I regretted later. But now, when I was working to control what I said, her words just hurt.

My mom waved a hand as though brushing away my words. "You need to spend more time with our dogs who get serious training. It just makes such a difference."

Lily knowing how I felt was all I cared about. But

my mom would never understand that. And this was why I could never ask her to put up a flyer about the shelter's foster program at the Pampered Puppy.

I'd done everything I could to hide the truth from my friends, but the fact was that my mom looked down on the shelter and nothing I said was going to change her mind.

4

The cafeteria was bustling as usual with friends talking, calling to each other across the tables, and bursting out into loud laughter. Sasha, Kim, Taylor, and I wove our way around stray backpacks and gave a wide berth to the food fight going on at Dennis Cartwright's table as we headed to our usual spot by a window along the back wall.

"Hey, guys," our friend Dana said when we arrived. "I brought cookies today." She, Emily, Naomi, and

Rachel sat at the table next to ours and we often shared food.

"Ooh, what kind?" Taylor asked, setting down her tray so she could accept the tin that Dana passed over.

"Lemon cornmeal," Emily answered. "And they're delicious."

Dana grinned. "I'm experimenting with recipes because my little sister wants a cookie birthday party this year."

"Smart kid," Taylor said, taking a cookie and giving me the tin. The cookies were golden with crisp tan edges and my mouth watered as I took one.

"Thanks," I said. I set mine on a napkin to save it for dessert.

"Yeah, I'm thinking my next party will be a cookie party too," Naomi said with a grin. "As long as Dana's doing the baking."

"Make sure you invite us," Sasha said.

Naomi gave her a thumbs-up and they turned back to their table as we dug into our food. Kim had her usual turkey sandwich, Taylor had her yogurt and granola, and Sasha had a salad. I was the only one who switched things up. Sometimes I got the hot lunch, but other times I brought leftovers in a thermos. Today I had last night's pork, eggplant, and rice, and the spicy scent greeted me as soon as I twisted off the top of the container.

"That smells good," Taylor said.

"Have a bite," I said, passing it to her. A lock of my hair slid out of the twist I'd created that morning. It was kind of falling apart, so while Taylor had my food I pulled it free and let my hair fall around my shoulders. Sometimes my styles were a little too ambitious.

Taylor scooped some out with her spoon. "Your mom is the best cook," she said after swallowing.

"She makes authentic Chinese food even though she grew up in California," I said proudly. My mom's cooking really was awesome. "Her mom taught her and now she's teaching me." So far she'd only taught me how to cut up meat and vegetables, but in Chinese cooking that was very important and over half the work.

"We have to sleep over at your house one day so we can have a true feast," Taylor said.

I nodded, but felt my body stiffen at the suggestion. The three of them had slumber parties most weekends, with awesome traditions like making milk shakes with mix-ins, talking club business, and the usual sleepover requirements like staying up late and sleeping in. So far I'd been to two and I knew at some point I'd have to host. I'd be happy to have Sasha, Taylor, and Kim see my home and eat the food my mom made, and meet my dad if he was around. But the problem was my mom: I knew she would insult the club and take it too far, like she always did. I could only imagine how much that would upset the other girls, and what if they decided I shouldn't be in the club anymore because of the things my mom said? "Speaking of sleepovers, I won't be around Saturday night," Kim said. "We're going to my cousin's wedding in Dayton."

"That sounds fun," Sasha said, spearing a cherry tomato.

"Yeah, it's twenties themed so at the reception they're teaching everyone dances like the jitterbug," Kim said.

"I'd love to see Matt doing the jitterbug," Taylor said with a grin. Matt was Kim's fifteen-year-old brother, who was definitely more comfortable on the athletic field than the dance floor.

Kim laughed. "Not likely," she said. She took a bite of her sandwich.

"I can't do a sleepover this weekend either," Sasha said. "I'm having extra dance rehearsals to get ready for our recital."

"I can't wait to see that," Kim said with a grin. One of the things I loved most about my new friends was the way they supported one another.

"Yeah, we'll be in the front row," Taylor said.

"Totally," I agreed.

"Bri, wait 'til you see how skilled Sasha is," Kim boasted. "She's going to be famous one day for sure."

It was another reminder that I was the outsider, the

only one who hadn't seen Sasha dance.

"Speaking of awesome skills, Bri, did you get a chance to work on the logo?" Taylor asked. And now I felt like part of things again.

"Yeah," I said, my face warming a bit as I pulled a folder out of my backpack. "I played around a little last night. If you guys don't like any of these I can keep working on more." I hadn't just played; I'd spent over two hours carefully creating and combining images that I felt represented the mood and tone of the club and the foster program. But I didn't want to act like it was a big deal in case Sasha, Kim, and Taylor hated them.

I passed Taylor the five concepts I'd finally decided on, then twisted my pendant nervously. It was a jade stone on a red string, which in China meant good luck. And hopefully it would mean the same thing here because I really wanted them to like my work.

"Bri, these are so good," Sasha said, looking up at me a minute later, impressed. She was holding my favorite design, the one that was a large tan paw print, inspired by Alice's T-shirt yesterday, with a small pink heart that fit right inside on the top left.

Her words made me swell with pride.

"Yeah, they really are," Kim agreed. She was looking at the one that had the cartoon figures of a dog and a human standing close together, the dog looking up at the person and the person looking down at the dog. "Bri, you're going to be famous too."

"I'm not sure there are famous graphic designers," I said with a happy grin.

"Then you'll be the first," Taylor said. "But there is a problem with these."

My spirits sank. "What?" I asked, feeling anxious.

Taylor grinned. "How are we ever going to choose just one?"

The Dog Club wasn't meeting that afternoon. Sasha had dance class, Taylor was going to her photography class, and Kim was headed to meet Anna for tutoring. That meant I was on my own and I decided to go to the Pampered Puppy to see if my mom needed help with anything. I disliked how she always put down our Dog Club in favor of the Pampered Puppy, but I was still proud of her and the business she had built. I knew how much hard work that took, and I also knew that even if she could be snobby about it, my mom genuinely adored dogs and wanted them well cared for.

The Pampered Puppy was in a converted Victorian house just off Main Street. The big front yard had perfectly manicured grass, and a big white sign with pink letters spelling out the name of the spa. The porch, painted a matching white, had little pink dog prints going up the steps to the front door. There was a reception area in front where Jon, the administrative assistant, sat behind a wooden desk. He grinned when I came in.

"What's up, Bri?" he asked.

"Not much," I said, smiling. Jon, like all the staff at the Pampered Puppy, was really nice.

The reception area had puffy pink chairs and frames with famous dog paintings. My favorite was the series of blue dog prints. That was the kind of art I hoped to make one day, though I had a long way to go before I'd be that good.

"Your mom's in with the big dogs," Jon said.

"Thanks, I'll go find her," I said.

The Pampered Puppy had two main rooms, one for small dogs and the other for big. Both rooms had hardwood floors that gleamed due to a thick protective clear gloss layer that was impenetrable to dog nails. The walls were painted a soothing light blue, and the rooms had top-quality dog beds and organic, all-natural dog toys stored in color-coded bins. The high-powered ventilation system, which kept everything smelling fresh and the air clean, hummed softly in the background as I headed into the big dog room.

"Hey, Bri," called Karen, one of the dog specialists who worked full time at the spa. She and all the other staff wore the same fitted lab coats as my mom, and for a moment I couldn't help comparing their sleek look to Alice with her baggy dog T-shirts, Caley with her wild outfits, Tim with his crazy hair, and the four of us who looked like, well, kids. Everyone here was trained and no one was under the age of twenty-one.

"Hi, Bun," my mom said from where she was squatting on the floor with a snowy white poodle.

I shot her a look. I didn't mind if she called me Bun at home, but out in public was another story.

"I mean, hello, Brianna," my mom said in an amused tone. "How nice to see you here."

I rolled my eyes. "Hi, Mom," I said as a caramel-colored cocker spaniel came over to sniff my shoes. "And hi there, Barney."

Barney nuzzled against my leg and I rubbed his butter-soft fur. He'd definitely been groomed earlier.

"See, he knows his name," my mom said proudly. "And watch this. Sit, Barney."

Barney sat instantly.

"Roll over," my mom said, coming over to us.

Barney immediately dropped to the floor and rolled over.

"Paw," my mom commanded, and Barney sat back up and offered a paw.

My mom reached into her coat pocket for a dog treat, the kind made with organic ingredients that cleaned the dog's teeth. She gave it to Barney, who gobbled it up, clearly happy with his reward.

"Very impressive," I told Barney.

"He behaves beautifully," my mom said. "Cocker spaniels are smart and his training started the minute we opened our doors. And you can see the results."

I definitely didn't want to go down this road again. "Is there anything I can do to help you out?" I asked.

"Let's see," my mom said, gazing around the room. "Sierra is out on her afternoon walk with Zia, Barney is going in for a training with Karen, and I'm working with Clarabelle. Scooter and Franz are having free play. Do you want to start a game of fetch with them?"

Scooter was a husky and one of my favorite dogs, while Franz was a spirited but well behaved golden retriever. "Yeah," I said, heading over to the toy bin shelf. I reached into the green one and pulled out a clean blue ball. It was pretty much the opposite of Boxer's chewed-up Frisbee.

"Franz and Scooter play with toys from the red container," my mom corrected.

With a sigh I reached into the red bin and pulled out what seemed to be the exact same blue ball. Sometimes the rules at the Pampered Puppy seemed silly.

But once I started playing fetch with Scooter and Franz, everything felt good again. Yes, there were a lot more rules at the Pampered Puppy; yes, it was fancier with a focus on training. But underneath all that they were just fun, snuggly dogs who liked to play and cuddle. Which was exactly the same as the dogs at the shelter, well trained or not.

If that was so obvious to me, why was it impossible for my mom to see it too?

5

It was one of those late fall afternoons that felt summery and the four of us had our coats unzipped as we strolled through town on the way to Dog Club, dogs prancing happily alongside us. After splitting up for pickups, we'd met for a twenty-minute run at the dog park, since it was so nice out, and now we were headed to the shelter.

"I can't believe it's going to be winter soon," Sasha said. She was walking Mr. S, Popsicle, and Humphrey.

"Does it get really cold here?" Taylor asked. She tugged gently on Coco's leash so that she would keep up. Coco liked to sniff everything we passed, which was annoying Waffles, who seemed eager to get to the club.

"Yes, freezing," the rest of us replied in unison, then laughed.

It was fun to be on the inside for once. Today I had Gus, Hattie, and Jinx, who already felt like she'd been part of the club forever. It was so much easier for dogs to fit in than people.

"Yikes, that sounds bad," Taylor said. "I think I'll miss the South when the first snowstorm hits." Taylor and her family had moved from North Carolina this past summer and that was what gave her words their soft drawl when she spoke. It wasn't a full-on Southern accent, more just a musical lilt.

"Yeah, but wait 'til you see how cute dogs are when they frolic in the snow," Kim pointed out. We were walking past Bundt Cake Bakery, the smell of fresh baked bread rich in the air. Missy, who stayed close to Kim, lifted her nose for an extra-long sniff.

"Yeah, and it will be Popsicle's first time seeing snow," Sasha said, grinning at the thought.

"Hattie's too," Kim said.

Taylor smiled. "That will be worth it," she said.

We passed Nimsey's Crafts and then the Rox, where we waved at Kim's mom who was at the hostess desk. Just then a colorful flyer stapled to a telephone booth caught my eye. I tugged gently on my dogs' leashes and stopped to take a closer look.

"What is that, Bri?" Taylor asked.

"It's for the town craft fair," I said as I skimmed it. "Two weeks from Saturday."

"Right, that happens every fall," Kim said. "It's a festival with booths where you can buy crafts and food, and a big art show in the town hall."

"There's also a stage for musical performances," Sasha said.

"That sounds great," Taylor said.

"Yeah, but the best part is that stores and businesses

can rent booths to sell art and merchandise," I said.

Sasha nodded, then suddenly her eyes got big. "Bri, you're brilliant!"

Kim's forehead crinkled. "I think you lost me."

"We can rent a booth for the dog shelter," I said excitedly. "To raise money and tell everyone who goes by about the fostering program."

Now Kim was nodding enthusiastically. "People come from all over and we can pass out flyers. That will really get the word out about the dogs needing temporary homes."

"And we can sell cute doggy things to raise money for the program and the shelter," Taylor finished. "Bri, you are brilliant."

Waffles barked as if in agreement. Or because he wanted us to get moving so he could play with his friends at the shelter. We started walking again and a few minutes later we'd arrived.

"Wait 'til you guys hear Bri's great idea," Taylor said as we trooped in.

"Lay it on us," Tim said. He was tossing a ball with

Tuesday, Boxer, and Gracie.

"Yeah, let's hear it," Caley said. She was on the floor playing a game of tug-of-war with Lily, but as soon as Lily saw me she ran over for a hug. Which made me feel just as good as Taylor's announcement.

"We need Alice too," Kim said. She'd already unleashed Missy, and while the rest of us were freeing our dogs she headed to Alice's office.

A moment later they came out together, Alice wearing one of my favorite T-shirts with a dog in the sun that said "Hot Dog."

"Hey, everybody," she said with a smile. Oscar, the soft gray shelter cat who thought he was a dog, twined around her ankles as Coco and Waffles went to greet Alice, then headed to play. "What's this fabulous idea?"

"Well, I saw a flyer for the town craft fair," I said. "And I thought we could rent a booth for the shelter. We can pass out our flyers for the foster program."

"And sell merchandise to raise money for the shelter and the foster program," Taylor added. Boxer brought his Frisbee over to her and she sent it sailing across the room. A crowd of dogs raced after it.

"I love it," Caley said approvingly. Humphrey and Missy were sniffing at a rubber bone and she went over to throw it for them.

"Yeah, it really is a great idea," Tim said.

"I agree," Alice said. "Smart thinking, Bri. It looks like you inherited your mother's instincts for good business."

That was a compliment for sure, though if Alice knew the things my mom said about *Alice*'s business, she might not smile at me so nicely. I shook the thought away.

"Now we just have to make those flyers," Alice went on.

"Bri has some great designs for the logo," Sasha said.

"Let's see," Caley said eagerly.

I pulled the folder out of my bag and passed around the pictures.

"These are wonderful," Alice said after looking

them over. She was holding the paw print one, and Boxer came over and tried to sniff it. Alice laughed and held it out of reach so he couldn't drool on it, but gave his ears a hearty scratch.

"Which one do you guys like best?" Caley asked.

"They're all great, but I think the paw print with the heart might be my favorite," Sasha said.

Kim was nodding. "Yeah, it's like when you see it you think dog and then love, which is exactly what we want people to think."

"Good point," Taylor agreed. "I vote for that one too."

"Same," Tim said, going back to play with Coco and Waffles, who had discovered the rubber bone.

"I like it too," Alice said, and Caley nodded. "But Bri, you're the artist—what do you think?"

I liked being called an artist. "The paw print has always been my favorite," I confessed.

"Then it's decided," Alice said. "I wrote up a description of the foster program so all that's left is figuring out the layout with the logo. Bri, can you help me with that?"

"Definitely," I said, happy to be asked.

Caley and Tim took a group of dogs out to play in the yard while Kim, Sasha, and Taylor played inside and I helped Alice finish the flyer. It looked slick and professional thanks to Alice's new color printer, and a half hour later we had a stack of papers ready to go.

"Bri, how many do you want for the Pampered Puppy?" Alice asked, making my chest clench up.

"Um, maybe one to put up on the bulletin board?" I could just find another place to post it so it wouldn't go to waste.

"Why don't you take a stack to keep on the reception desk too?" Alice asked. "That way people who are interested can take one home." She was handing me a pile of flyers so it wasn't even like it was a question.

"Sure," I said, a sinking feeling in my stomach. Where could I put all these flyers? Because I certainly couldn't ask my mom to give them away at the

Pampered Puppy. Lily had been playing with Tuesday, but as though she sensed my anxiety she came over to lean against me, looking up with concern.

"She's really bonded to you," Alice observed.

I gently stroked the soft fur on the top of Lily's head. "It's mutual," I said.

"I'll take some flyers for the Rox," Kim said, coming over, Missy tagging along behind her.

"And give me a bunch for my mom's law firm," Sasha said. "My mom was excited when I told her about the foster program."

"My dad too," Taylor said. "He'll want to help since I don't think we can foster a dog. Jasmine is allergic." Taylor had two other sisters besides Anna, twins Jasmine and Tasha, who were juniors in high school.

I hadn't even thought about participating in the program until just now. And slowly an idea began to bloom in my mind. What if I was somehow able to get my mom to agree to take in Lily? I knew my mom felt as strongly as Alice did about dogs finding homes instead of being put down in shelters. Fostering was something my mom would believe in. Of course, taking in an older dog like Lily wouldn't be her first choice. But if I got her to give it a try, my mom could see how wonderful all dogs were, not just dogs with tons of training. Lily was so special—my mom had to see that. If she loved Lily half as much as I did, maybe we'd even get to adopt her. And that would be bliss!

Lily licked my hand and I reached down and hugged her. "I'm going to try to talk my mom into fostering Lily," I announced. Just saying the words out loud felt great.

"Awesome," Taylor said, and Kim gave me a thumbs-up.

"Lily would love that," Alice said, smiling down fondly at Lily. "She has a good life at the shelter, but I know she'd adore being at home with you. I've noticed how she watches you when you're here."

That made me feel terrific. The only thing was that I had to somehow talk my mom into it. And that was going to be more of a challenge than anyone at Dog Club knew.

The back door burst open and Boxer raced in, followed by Coco, Waffles, Hattie, Tuesday, Popsicle, Daisy, and Tim, whose cheeks were red from running. Last came Caley and Gus. All the dogs were panting happily.

"We came back in because inspiration struck," Tim said grandly.

Caley rolled her eyes.

"It's a day of great ideas because you guys will never believe my genius plan for our booth at the craft fair," Tim said dramatically.

"You might want to be sitting down for it," Caley said. "But not because it's good."

"She's jealous," Tim said, waving his hand dismissively. "Since it's not just going to make the club money, it's going to make doggy basketball a worldwide sensation."

"This I have to hear," Alice said with a grin. The

rest of us were nodding as we played with the dogs.

"I'm going to create a beginner's video to doggy basketball, that comes with a ball, the video, and a basket," Tim said. "It's going to be called *Legendary Coach Tim Sanchez's Dog Basketball for Beginners*. An instant best seller, am I right?"

I could see that Alice was trying to stifle a laugh.

"I already pointed out the cost of making the video would probably be more than we'd make selling them," Caley said drily. "And how it's not really a game that requires a lot of instruction. I'm not even sure what you'd put on a video."

"Pointers from an experienced coach," Tim said, like it was obvious. "I'll share all my coaching secrets." Hattie had come up to him with a tennis ball, which he sent bouncing across the room for her.

"It might work if it starred Bri since she always beats you," Caley said with a teasing grin. She was petting Jinx.

"That's cold," Tim said. "Though unfortunately

true. Hey, Bri, do you want to star in my video?"

"I think I'm more comfortable behind the scenes," I said, grinning. I knew as well as anyone that my winning streak was due more to luck than anything else. Doggy basketball was fun, but not exactly a real, coachable sport.

"Okay, maybe the whole concept needs some work," Tim said with a sigh. "But if we're not going to sell my awesome videos to raise money, what are we going to sell?"

"Good question," Sasha said. "We want really unique, fun things that people won't be able to resist buying, and that show the spirit of the Dog Club."

"And that aren't too expensive to make," Kim added. She was sitting on the floor, Missy in her lap and Humphrey snuggled beside them. Taylor noticed how cute it was and took out her camera for a quick shot. We never posted photos of us on the blog or website, since both were public, but all of us had Dog Club pictures up in our rooms and as backgrounds on our phones and computers. This would be a great one for Kim.

Thinking about Taylor's awesome photos gave me an idea. "What about a calendar?" I asked. "Every month can be a different picture of the shelter dogs."

"And we have tons of great shots thanks to Taylor," Sasha said, excited by the idea.

"I bet calendars aren't too expensive to print up," Kim said. "And we can have our logo and information about the shelter on them too, so they'll be pretty and also be an ad for the shelter."

"I think a lot of businesses would put them up, like in their lobbies and waiting rooms," Taylor said.

"My mom totally would," Sasha said. "Her office has one up now from one of the organizations she represents, so I know she'd put up ours in January."

"We always have at least one up at the Rox," Kim said. "Right by the register so everyone who comes in sees it."

"And think how many people love cute dog photos," Sasha said, snuggling Gracie, who had trotted over to her. "With Taylor's great shots I bet they'll sell out."

"See, now *that* is a good idea," Caley said to Tim. "Something easy to make that people will actually want to buy."

Tim threw up his arms in mock dismay. "It's sad how no one here recognizes true entrepreneurial spirit when it's standing right in front of them."

We all cracked up at that.

But then I had another idea. "Hey, maybe the calendar could be themed, like 'dogs at play,'" I said. "We can have pictures of dogs chasing toys or running around in a game of dog tag."

"And a whole month dedicated to doggy basketball," Tim exclaimed.

"Yeah," I said, grinning again.

Tim gave me a thumbs-up. "Now *that* is a great idea."

6

"What yummy leftovers do you have today?" Taylor asked over the din of the cafeteria.

I smiled as I twisted off the cap of my thermos. "My mom's spicy sesame noodles," I said. "Try some."

Just as I reached over to pass it to her, a group of boys went by and one of them jostled my arm, nearly causing me to drop my thermos. I turned, ready to yell at him.

"Sorry," he said quickly, holding up both hands. Clearly it was an honest mistake.

In the past I would have taken his head off anyway, but now I took a deep breath, calming myself before I responded. "No problem," I said.

"Nicely done," Taylor said, giving me a thumbs-up. I smiled, appreciating that she noticed my efforts to control my temper. And then I handed her the thermos.

"Delish," Taylor said after taking a bite. "Hey, what did your mom say about fostering Lily?"

My chest tightened at her words. "I haven't asked her yet," I said. When I'd gotten home last night my mom had been distracted about a meeting she'd had with her accountant, so it hadn't been the best time to approach the fostering idea. Not that I was planning to ask outright, of course. My mom would have to be softened up first. The problem was that I wasn't sure how to do that, though I wasn't going to tell my friends that.

But Sasha must have noticed the way I was biting my lip. "It can be hard to ask for something you want so much," she said. "I had to badger my mom forever before she let me get Mr. S."

"Yeah, you really worked for that," Kim remembered. "But Bri's mom will probably be happy to foster Lily, right? I mean she obviously loves dogs since she opened a doggy day care."

"Um, I'm not sure," I said, scrambling for a reason why. A reason that I could say to my friends, that is.

But Sasha saved me. "Just because Bri's mom works with dogs doesn't mean she wants to own one," she said. "Maybe she wants a break from animals at night. Or maybe she's like my mom and gets fussy about keeping a clean house."

"She definitely cares about a clean house," I said. That was totally true. I wasn't sure about her wanting a break from dogs, though. Back in DC we'd lived in a building that did not allow pets. And when we first got to Roxbury Park my mom had been busy setting up her business while we settled in. But she was such a dog lover that I suspected she'd be happy to take one in.

The catch was that her idea of what kind of dog to get would be different from mine.

"I can give you some pointers then," Sasha said. "Guys, remember how I told my mom I wanted a skunk?"

Taylor and Kim burst out laughing. I pasted a smile on my face, trying to cover up my fourth-wheel feeling and confusion about why Sasha had wanted a *skunk*.

"It was my strategy to convince my mom to agree to getting me a pet," Sasha explained. "I knew if I asked her for a hamster, she'd say no. But if I asked for a skunk and then a hamster, the hamster would seem like no big deal."

"Smart," I said, nodding thoughtfully.

"So maybe you can do something like that with your mom," Sasha finished.

"That could work," I agreed, thinking about it. The problem was that my mom would probably think the worst option out there *was* an older shelter dog like Lily.

"Another way you can go is by talking about how

you're ready to take on more responsibility and a dog would be a great way to do that," Kim said. "That worked for Sasha too."

"Yeah, it was showing my mom how much I wanted a dog and that I could handle taking care of one," Sasha said. Then she giggled. "But it didn't go so well at first."

She and the others started reminiscing about some kind of baking fiasco, but this time I wasn't worried about being a fourth wheel.

This time I was planning how to approach my mom. And my friends had given me just the idea I needed.

Saturday morning the four of us were meeting on Main Street to put up flyers for the fostering program. It was a chilly day and I had to run back to put on a heavier jacket, which made me a little late. But Taylor was walking up just as I approached Kim, Sasha, and Mr. S in front of Nimsey's Crafts.

"You guys, it's freezing," Taylor exclaimed. She and I both bent down to pet Mr. S.

Sasha laughed. "This is nothing," she said as a brisk wind scattered some fallen leaves on the sidewalk around us. "Wait 'til January."

"The worst is February," Kim said as Taylor shuddered. "That's when it feels like it's been cold forever and spring will never come."

"We'll have to change our sleepover tradition from milk shakes to cocoa," Taylor said.

"Hmm, that's not a bad idea," Sasha said. "We could make hot chocolate drinks with cinnamon or caramel."

"Or both," I said with a grin.

"That's what I'm talking about," Taylor said, leaning over to give me a high five.

Mrs. Washington, Gus's owner, drove by and honked in greeting. We all waved back. Another typical Roxbury Park moment that gave me a warm, cozy feeling despite the cool weather.

"Okay, let's get going," Kim said. She had the flyers and we'd all brought staplers and masking tape. "We want the town covered so everyone knows about the fostering program."

"Should we split up?" Sasha asked. She was twirling the end of Mr. S's leash absently.

"Yeah, that'll be more efficient," Kim said. "Taylor, you and Bri take the other side of the street plus the community center. Sash and I will take this side and the park."

"Perfect," Taylor agreed. "Meet you back in front of Sugar and Spice."

"How about *inside* Sugar and Spice?" Sasha suggested. "We'll have earned some candy after all that hard work."

"It's a plan," Taylor said eagerly.

"Is Jasmine working there today?" Sasha asked. Taylor's older sister Jasmine had a part-time job at the candy store, which seemed like the best kind of job ever.

Taylor shook her head. "She and Tasha are taking an SAT class on Saturdays."

Kim wrinkled her nose. "That doesn't sound as fun as working at Sugar and Spice."

Taylor laughed. "That's what Jasmine said. But she wants to be a doctor so she's serious about school stuff."

Kim and Sasha crossed at the corner. Taylor and I strolled down the street putting up flyers on every bulletin board, telephone pole, and lamppost. We went inside each store and restaurant and asked to put up flyers there too. With Roxbury Park being Roxbury Park, everyone was happy to help out.

"So have you asked your mom about Lily yet?" Taylor asked after we'd hung our second-to-last paper and were headed toward Sugar and Spice.

"Tonight," I said. "I had to make sure my plan was foolproof before springing it on her."

"Smart," Taylor said, the wind blowing her braids and making the beads clink pleasantly. "Parents need to be handled carefully when it comes to a big change."

"Totally," I agreed. Though she had no idea how careful I had to be with my mom.

We headed to Sugar and Spice and were surprised to see Kim and Sasha standing outside.

"Don't tell me you're canceling our candy stop," Taylor said, a fake scowl on her face.

Sasha laughed. "No way," she said. "We earned our candy today. But Kim and I had this really good idea we wanted to tell you guys about first."

"Does it involve candy?" Taylor asked.

"Yes," Kim said, grinning.

"Okay, then you have my full attention," Taylor said, smiling and brushing a braid off her face.

"When we were done putting up our flyers we were walking over here and talking about all the great treats they have at Sugar and Spice," Sasha began.

"And how much everyone in town loves their candy," Kim added.

A group of boys on skateboards were heading toward us, so we moved to the side to let them pass.

"Especially since the new owners have added all kinds of fabulous combinations like chocolate peanut butter squares with crispy rice," Sasha went on.

"Oh, those were so good," I agreed, remembering the day a few weeks ago when we'd stopped by the store and discovered them.

"I loved the mint chocolate bars with crushed Oreos," Taylor added dreamily.

We all nodded.

"So we were thinking," Kim went on, "that we should ask the new owners if they'd be interested in making candy for us to sell at the craft fair."

"Oh, that's a terrific idea," I exclaimed.

"Downright brilliant," Taylor agreed.

Kim and Sasha exchanged a glance and then looked at Taylor. "We were hoping you'd do the pitch," Kim said sheepishly.

"You're the perfect choice because you're so comfortable talking to everyone," Sasha added.

For a second I felt stung that they hadn't asked me. But then I remembered I didn't exactly have the best history of speaking nicely to people. "Yeah, you'll do a great job," I agreed. "Plus everyone loves your Southern accent."

"Well, when y'all butter me up like this, how can I say no?" Taylor asked in an exaggerated drawl that cracked us up.

Then she opened the door to Sugar and Spice, the scent of chocolate, toffee, and lemon swirling around us in a delicious cloud as we trooped inside. My mouth was watering before the door closed fully behind us. The store was small but cheery, with candy in all shapes and sizes covering the counters, artfully arranged on small tables and set out in a big glass display case next to the register. The walls had a bright mural of a candy village, with gingerbread houses, gummy people, a river of hot chocolate, and rainbow flower gardens made of sour balls and jawbreakers. The back wall and door were decked out with rainbow polka dots.

"Hi, welcome," a woman said as she walked out of the back kitchen, a tray held in her hand. She wore her long black hair in a complicated twist that I immediately decided to try to re-create for school on Monday.

"Want to try a new candy my sister and I just whipped up?" she asked us. "They're essentially mini s'mores—chocolate marshmallow squares with a graham cracker crust and little toffee chunks baked in."

We each took one and I bit into mine immediately. The rich chocolate, buttery toffee, and fluffy marshmallow were heavenly, the graham adding just the right amount of crunch.

"Fabulous," Taylor proclaimed with a big thumbs-up. We all nodded in agreement. "And actually, we kind of wanted to talk to you about your fabulous candy and offer you guys a business proposition."

The woman set down the tray. "Um, okay," she said, sounding surprised. She probably didn't get business propositions every day, especially from middle school students. "Let me just call my sister."

"I'm here." A second woman popped out of the kitchen. She had dark eyes and tan skin like her sister, but she wore her thick black hair in a sleek bob. "What's up?"

"We are the Roxbury Park Dog Club," Taylor said, then introduced us each by name.

"I'm Carmen Lopez and this is my sister, Marisol," the woman with the long hair said. "What kind of business proposition do you guys have in mind?"

"And what is the Roxbury Park Dog Club?" Marisol added.

The four of us filled the sisters in on the club, the craft fair, and our new fostering program.

"I wish I could take in one of the dogs," Carmen said wistfully. "But my husband is allergic."

"And my building doesn't allow pets," Marisol said. "I'm sorry we can't help out more."

We exchanged a look. "Actually, you can," Taylor said, straightening up for her big moment. "We were hoping you might consider creating a candy for us to sell in our booth, something like little chocolates in the shapes of dogs to go with the theme of our booth."

The sisters made eye contact in a way that let you know they were having some kind of unspoken communication, and after a moment Marisol nodded once.

"We'd love to if we can afford to do it," Carmen said. "Let us crunch some numbers and then get back to you."

"Okay," Taylor said. I could tell she was disappointed and I was too.

"We like the idea a lot," Marisol reassured us. "But our business is just starting out and we have to make sure we have the funds to do it before we commit."

"That makes sense," Sasha said. "Here's our last flyer so you know how to find us." She passed the sheet of paper to Marisol, who immediately hung it behind the register.

"Thanks," Taylor said, grinning. At the very least they were advertising for us and that was something.

"And I need to take some of these home for my family," Kim said, gesturing to the tray of s'mores bars. "I think I can get Matt to do my chores for a week if I give him a couple of these."

"Good idea," I agreed. My mom had a sweet tooth and the candy would help my case tonight.

Marisol helped us each pack up exactly how much we wanted in rainbow polka-dotted cardboard boxes that said "Sugar and Spice" in swirly letters. We paid and then she handed us each a lemon lollipop. "For the road," she said with a smile.

"Fabulous, thanks," Taylor said, speaking for all of us.

"We'll be in touch," Carmen called as we headed out.

"I hope they say yes," Taylor said once we were outside. The air had gotten even colder and she hugged her arms around herself.

"Me too," I agreed. "And you did a great job pitching it."

"Totally," Sasha agreed, taking the wrapper off her lolly and popping it in her mouth.

"I'm off to get ready for the wedding," Kim said, twirling her candy between her hands. "But this was a really good morning."

"Definitely," Taylor agreed.

We walked down Main Street, which was now extra colorful with all our flyers. At the corner we stopped to say good-bye.

"Good luck tonight, Bri," Taylor said, reaching over to squeeze my hand.

Kim and Sasha glanced at me questioningly.

"I'm going to ask my mom if we can take Lily in," I explained.

"Oh, I have my fingers crossed," Sasha said. The wind blew a stray curl into her face and she brushed it aside.

"Me too," Kim said.

"Thanks," I said, meaning it.

Because I knew I'd need all the luck I could get if I had any hope of convincing my mom to agree to my dream of fostering Lily.

7

My approach for getting my
mom to agree to foster Lily
was simple, thanks to my
friends. They had reminded
me that the key to a convincing argument was using
something my mom really cared about. For Sasha's
mom that had been responsibility. For my mom it was
being prepared. So I'd spent hours creating and printing
up my plans for Lily's care, with a daily schedule and a
weekly one. I'd included the things my mom valued,

like training and a proper diet. I took Lily's individual needs into account and focused on things that mattered most to my mom. All in all, it was pretty foolproof.

But just to be safe I had a second layer to my approach, and that was to get my dad on my side. Which probably wouldn't be too hard. My dad always felt a bit guilty about how much he was away, which was why he got me such great presents. So when I video chatted with him tonight, I planned to let him know the one present I wanted more than anything: Lily.

With my dad on my side and my carefully prepared strategy, not to mention the candy from Sugar and Spice, there was no way my mom could turn me down.

And to add extra security, I did all my chores in record time and offered to clean up after dinner so my mom could relax before my dad called. When I finally sat down in front of the computer in my mom's home office to chat with my dad, I was ready to go.

"Hey, sweetie," he said, his voice warm. As always my heart clenched up just a bit. I really missed having him around, and seeing his face on the computer screen, no matter how big his smile, was just not the same. "How are you?"

"Pretty good," I said.

"What did you do today?" he asked, giving me the perfect opening for the conversation I wanted to have.

"Remember how I told you about the fostering program the Roxbury Park Shelter is starting?" I asked.

My dad nodded—he always remembered everything I told him.

"Today Kim, Sasha, Taylor, and I went all over town putting up flyers to let everyone know about it," I said.

"It's nice you had a fun activity with your friends," my dad said.

It *was* nice, but my dad was picking up on the wrong part of the story.

"Yeah, it was good," I said, but then went on quickly. "And there was a lot of interest in the program. People really want to help find homes for dogs, so they won't have to be killed in shelters."

My dad nodded. "It's a great thing you kids and Alice are doing," he said.

Now *that* was the right part of the story.

"Yes, and it made me realize that I want to do more too," I said, then took a deep breath. "Dad, do you think we could foster a dog?"

My dad's eyebrows scrunched for a moment, but then he nodded. "Yes, I think that's a great idea. Your mom and I have discussed when we'd get a dog, and we thought we'd wait until you really wanted one. And I like the idea of doing it this way, helping out a dog in need."

"Awesome," I said, grinning so wide my cheeks felt tight. This had gone even better than I'd hoped! "And I know just the dog I want."

My dad pressed his hands together. "Well, your mom is going to want some say in that," he said. "She has contacts at a lot of places that rescue dogs and she may prefer to get one of those."

With that my grin was gone. "But I want to help out a dog from the shelter," I said. Actually I kind of whined, but I couldn't help it. How could my dad side with my mom at a time like this?

"If it's okay with your mom, it's fine with me," my dad said. "I'll love any dog we take in."

It was true, he would. The problem was, would my mom?

We finished up our chat and while my mom had her talk with my dad, I reviewed my argument for taking in Lily. I was determined to convince my mom, even without help from my dad.

"Want some tea?" I asked as soon as she was off the computer. "And some treats from Sugar and Spice?" I already had the hot water and a plate of the s'mores squares ready.

"Sure, that sounds nice," my mom said. Her eyes were always a bit sad after she said good-bye to my dad. I knew she missed him as much as I did.

I got our tea ready, using her favorite: dried chrysanthemum flowers that my dad brought back from China. We sat down at the table and I stirred sugar into mine while my mom blew gently on hers and then took a sip.

"Thanks, sweetie," my mom said. "This is relaxing after a long day."

"Try these too," I said, pushing the plate toward her. "They're really good."

My mom picked one up and took a small bite, then closed her eyes, savoring it. "This is delicious," she said, popping the rest of it in her mouth. "Thanks for bringing them home." Her voice was muffled from the candy.

"Anytime," I said. "And I actually had something I wanted to ask you."

My mom nodded, almost as though she had been expecting that. Maybe my efforts to butter her up had been a bit too obvious. But there was no worrying about that now.

"Alice has started this really great program to foster dogs," I said, my words coming out a bit rushed. "Some shelters nearby have contacted her to ask if she has room for any more dogs, dogs that haven't been adopted and will be put to sleep soon."

My mom's mouth pinched up at that.

"The thing is, after all the great publicity the Dog Club has been bringing to the shelter, it's filled to capacity and has a waiting list," I went on, turning my cup around in my hands. "Which is why Alice thought of fostering."

"It's a smart idea," my mom said, pausing to take another bite of s'mores square. "It can buy time for an animal who is in danger of being put down. And often families that foster fall in love with the dog and want to adopt it."

She had just said the perfect thing.

"Yeah, exactly," I said. "And that's why I thought we should take in one of the dogs. There's a dog at the shelter that I love. Her name is Lily and she's very obedient. She could also use a bit more training, so I thought we would be the perfect family to take her in." I pulled out the plan I had typed up and pointed to the first page. "This is a tentative schedule for Lily, when she'd eat and when I'd take her out for walks."

My mom looked down at the paper, nodding as she read. When she was done I handed her the next sheet.

"This is a training itinerary," I said. "I was hoping

you'd help me with it since you're the real expert."

My mom didn't quite smile at that but the corners of her mouth quirked up just a bit, which I took as a good sign.

"Lily sits and stays when you tell her to," I continued. "So she's clearly trainable. I think with the right instruction she'll learn just as well as the dogs at the Pampered Puppy."

This time the corners of my mom's mouth turned down a bit, so I went on, giving her my final argument. "I really love Lily," I said. "And she loves me. I don't think I've ever wanted anything as much as I want Lily to come live with us, at least for a little while." My voice broke the tiniest bit on the last words because it was true: I wanted this more than anything. "Please, Mom, let's foster Lily."

"Bun, your heart is in the right place," my mom said. "And I love the idea of us fostering a dog. It's worthy and important work." She stopped to sip some tea.

I nodded and held my breath as I waited for the final part of her response.

"But I just don't think an older shelter dog is right for us," she said, setting her mug down.

"But—" I began.

My mom held up a hand. "Let me finish," she said. "I know you love working with this dog at Dog Club, but here at home it would be different. Training her would take more time and energy than either of us have. And she's lived in the shelter for some time. It would be a big adjustment for her, and who knows what kind of bad behavior would result from that. And honestly, Bun—" She paused to rest her hand on mine. "If she's been in the shelter so long, it's likely that there's something wrong with her."

"There's nothing wrong with Lily," I burst out. "She's sweet and loving and listens to commands. She'd adore living at home with us, I'm sure of it."

"I know that's how you feel, but I've worked with dogs longer than you've been alive," my mom said. "I know there are hidden problems with dogs of this sort."

"Lily's not a *sort*," I said, trying not to yell. "She's

one dog who is awesome. If you'd just give her a chance I know you'd see that."

My mom pressed her fingertips together and studied my face for a moment. Then she sighed. "Or maybe you will finally see what I mean about how challenging it is to work with older dogs."

I winced slightly at the insult, but was my mom maybe, possibly, agreeing to take Lily?

"Okay, Bun, we can foster this dog," my mom said.

I leaped out of my chair and threw my arms around her.

"It's just for a few weeks," my mom said, laughing a bit at my enthusiasm. "And I think you'll finally understand what I keep trying to tell you about older dogs."

She said "older dogs" the way someone might say "this infestation of cockroaches," but I didn't care. Lily was coming home with me and nothing mattered more than that!

8

"So this is it," Taylor said as the four of us left school a few days later. The sky was gray and a light rain was falling, but nothing could dampen my mood because today was the day I was bringing Lily home.

"Yeah," I said, grinning. It was pretty much the same grin I'd had ever since my mom said yes. I just couldn't stop smiling at the thought of waking up every day with Lily, being greeted by her every afternoon after school, and snuggling with her every night. "My mom signed all the papers for Alice and I have them here in my bag." I patted my tie-dyed backpack.

"And you have all the supplies?" Sasha asked. She had a bright red umbrella that kept bumping into Kim's dark blue one as they walked.

I nodded. "Yup. I have the leash and collar all ready. And we got food and dishes and a dog bed over the weekend." I decided not to mention that we'd gotten organic dog food and a pet bed with all natural fibers because it seemed a bit silly. But once my mom had agreed to let us take Lily, I was happy to go along with all her ideas about the best ways to care for a dog. "And we got a bunch of toys too."

"You should ask Alice if you can bring one or two of Lily's favorite balls from the shelter," Kim suggested, sidestepping a puddle. "That way Lily will have something familiar with her in her new home."

"Great idea," I agreed, loving the sound of "new home." Of course it was just temporary, for now. We had simply agreed to foster Lily. But I had my fingers crossed that we would be one of the many families to fall in love with our foster dog and make her a permanent member of the family.

We separated at the corner to get our club pups and I headed to Coco's house. Once she was leashed and ready to go we walked two wet blocks to Waffles's house, where she ran in happy circles as soon as we got in the door.

"We're happy to see you too," I told her as I snapped her leash on. I couldn't help thinking that at the very next club meeting we'd have an extra dog to pick up: Lily!

When I walked into the shelter a few minutes later Lily raced over to greet me. "Today's a big day," I told her, rubbing her head for a moment before freeing Coco and Waffles from their leashes. "You're coming to live with me."

Lily barked as though she understood and then raced off to chase the red rubber ball Caley was throwing for her, Boxer, Jinx, and Tuesday. Maybe that was one of the toys I should ask Alice about. I pulled the paperwork out of my backpack and then went over to Alice's office. Her door was open and she waved me in with a smile.

"Are you all ready?" she asked me.

"I really am," I said, sitting in the slightly sagging chair next to Alice's desk and handing her the dog foster care agreement. "We have all the supplies we need for Lily." I twisted the end of my French braid around my fingertips.

Alice nodded as she skimmed the papers. "I'm sure you and your mom got her everything." She looked up and smiled. "It's wonderful your family is doing this."

"Yeah, I'm so excited about it," I said, nearly bouncing in my seat. "And my dad said he can't wait to meet Lily when he gets home in a few weeks."

"Super," Alice said. She leaned back in her chair and smoothed her T-shirt that said "Keep Calm and Walk the Dog." "Do you have any questions?"

"Just one," I said. "Can I take a couple of Lily's shelter toys home with us so she has something familiar with her?"

"What a lovely idea," Alice said, nodding. "Absolutely."

"It was Kim's suggestion," I said, wanting to give credit where it was due.

"She was smart to think of it," Alice said, standing up. "And you were smart to take it."

We headed back into the big room where Tim and Taylor were tossing tennis balls to Boxer, Coco, Waffles, Jinx, Gracie, and Gus. Caley and Hattie were playing tug-of-war with a blue rubber bone while Kim and Sasha were playing fetch with Mr. S, Popsicle, Lily, Tuesday, and Daisy. Missy and Humphrey were exploring the far corner of the room where a pile of toys was set out. The sounds of laughter, happy barking, and dog nails skidding on the floor made me smile as Lily whizzed past.

"Just another day of Dog Club," Alice said, chuckling

as Boxer nearly ran her over.

"Sorry about that," Taylor said, trotting over to us.

"Dogs should run, that's half the reason we have the club," Alice pointed out cheerfully.

"Good point," Taylor said.

Jinx pranced up and dropped a tennis ball at Taylor's feet. Taylor picked it up and lobbed it across the room, a crowd of dogs in hot pursuit.

"It's always a bit crowded on rainy days," Sasha said, coming over to us. "But I kind of like it when we're together all cozy like this."

Alice nodded as we watched Boxer steal the ball out from under Jinx's paws and sail away triumphantly. "Me too," she said.

"Definitely," I agreed. I liked Dog Club no matter how it came, with its warm chaos and homey feel. Though for a second I couldn't help thinking how horrified my mom would be if she walked in right now. This was definitely way more "helter-skelter" than the Pampered Puppy on its most active day.

The phone rang and Alice went into her office to answer it. A moment later she stuck her head out. "Sasha, it's for you," she said. "Carmen Lopez from Sugar and Spice."

Kim, Taylor, and I exchanged an excited look as a beaming Sasha flew in to take the call. But a few minutes later her smile was gone as she trudged out of the office. "Carmen said they'd love to help, but they just can't afford to give away a bunch of candy," she said with a sigh.

"I guess that makes sense," I said, thinking of my mom and how hard it was for small businesses to make ends meet, even without giving away free things.

"Yeah, but selling candy at our booth was such a good idea," Taylor moaned. "Everyone in town would have bought some."

We all nodded at that. It was such a shame they couldn't help us. And what would we do instead? Handing out flyers was great, but selling fun things like candy would get the word out about the club and the foster program in a whole new way. And that was what we needed.

Caley and Tim had just started up a game of doggy tag. Most of the dogs joined in, but Missy came over and leaned against Kim, who immediately sat so that Missy could get on her lap. We sat too, leaning up against the wall, out of the way of the game. A moment later Humphrey was lying down with a sigh next to Taylor while Jinx, clearly tuckered out, came to cuddle with Sasha. And then Lily came and climbed on my lap like she owned it.

"She is so your dog," Kim said with a grin. I wrapped my arms around Lily and buried my face in her soft fur. She really was mine, and hopefully my mom would see it.

"The thing is, what else are we going to be able to sell at the booth?" Sasha asked, getting back to the problem at hand while she gently stroked Jinx's ears. "The calendars are great, but we need more than that and I don't know how much we want to spend."

"That's a good point," Kim said. "We can't afford to buy candy or anything else really cool ourselves—we'd barely make a profit."

For a moment we sat in gloomy silence. But then Caley came over. Her cheeks were pink from running and she brushed back a lock of hair that had fallen out of her bun. "I have an idea for you guys," she said, sitting down on the floor across from us. "When we're doing plays at the high school, we earn the money for the programs by selling advertising space. And I think you guys should do the same thing. What if you asked businesses to make products for you to sell and they could put their logos on the product too?"

"So we'd ask the Lopez sisters to make candy that advertised their business *and* ours?" Kim clarified, a smile starting to spread across her face.

"Exactly," Caley said. "That way they aren't just donating to you guys but they're also investing in advertising for Sugar and Spice."

"That is *such* a good idea," Sasha said admiringly.

"Unlike, say, a doggy basketball video, right?" Caley asked, looking up at Tim, who was running by.

"I heard that and I'm deeply wounded," he called, sounding slightly out of breath.

Caley got up to join back in the game.

"I'm going to call Carmen and tell her our new proposition right now," Sasha said, standing up and heading back to Alice's office.

Kim, Taylor, and I stood up too, just as Popsicle bounded up to me, a green ball in her mouth, which she dropped at my feet. I gave it a toss and watched as a group of dogs, including Lily, *my* Lily, raced after it.

This time when Sasha came out of the office she looked cheerful. "Carmen said she'd talk to Marisol but that it sounded like a smart business plan."

"So she'll call us back?" Taylor asked as Boxer zipped by.

"Yeah, in a couple of days, after they crunch numbers again," Sasha said. "And since that's all we can do for now, I say we play some doggy tag!"

I was more than ready to have some quality dog time. "Watch out," I called, scooping up the ball and charging across the room. "Because this game just got serious!"

An hour and a half later the last dog had been picked up from Dog Club. That is, the last dogs except for Mr. S and Lily. I'd spent the last twenty minutes brushing Lily so that my mom would see how pretty she was. Now all I had to do was get her home!

"This is so great," Taylor said, squeezing my arm.

"It's very exciting," Alice agreed.

"Look at her," Caley said with a smile. We all gazed at Lily, who was on the floor biting the blue rubber bone. "She has no idea something fabulous is about to happen."

"You ready, Bri?" Tim asked.

I loved that they were all staying to see Lily and me off.

"I'm ready," I said, pulling out Lily's new green

leash with the matching green collar. The red ball and a plastic chew toy in the shape of a hamburger, another of Lily's favorites, were already in my bag.

I called Lily over and she bounded up at once. She stood still as I put on her new collar and leash and then looked up at me, slightly confused but clearly trusting, as I led her toward the door.

"You're coming home with me," I told her.

Lily seemed to accept this as the club gathered around to say good-bye.

"See you at the next club meeting," Tim said, patting Lily on the back while Caley rubbed her ears.

"And we'll see you on the walk to the club," Sasha said, with Mr. S beside her.

"Have fun in your new home," Taylor said. Then she grinned at me. "And have fun with your Lily."

"I will," I said, feeling so full of joy I thought I might explode.

Taylor pulled out her camera and began snapping photos.

"Be your sweet, good self," Alice told Lily. I saw a flicker of sadness in her eyes and knew that she would miss Lily, even though finding dogs homes was what she worked for.

I just hoped more than anything that this would be Lily's home, her real home, forever.

We headed out into the cloudy twilight. The rain had stopped but the air was chilly and damp.

"Let's go, Lily," I said.

Lily glanced back at the shelter, unsure of what was happening. But then she looked up at me, gave a short bark, and we were on our way.

And a few minutes later we were walking up the front path of my house. "This is where you'll be staying, hopefully from now on," I told Lily as I fumbled for my keys. "We have yummy food and a snug place for you to sleep," I told her. "And lots of toys."

When I opened the door Lily hesitated, as though wondering if she was really supposed to come in.

"Yes, this is just where you should be," I reassured

her. My stomach was full of happy, fizzy bubbles as Lily came in behind me, then began the serious business of sniffing everything in sight.

It was even more awesome than I'd hoped to have her here!

"This is the living room," I told Lily, starting a tour so she could get to know everything. "Here's the sofa where you will not be allowed to sit. But we have a dog bed for you right here, so you can watch TV with us and hang out in here too," I went on.

Lily was very interested in her new bed. She stepped into it, circled a few times, and then bit it.

"That's for sleeping, not eating," I said, laughing. "You'll get dinner in a minute, but first let's go to my room."

Lily agreeably got off her bed and followed me up the stairs.

"This is my mom and dad's room," I said as we passed the first door. "You'll meet my mom tonight and my dad in a few weeks. He'll see you tonight when we video chat, though, and I know he's going to love you."

Lily stopped to inspect the doorway.

"Let's stay out of there for now," I said. "I want to show you where you'll sleep at night with me."

I walked past the bathroom and opened the door to my room. Lily marched in and began sniffing my desk, bookcase, and closet. I gave her the shelter toys and she chewed them both for a moment, then kept the ball in her mouth as she explored. While she checked things out I put my stuff away and took a minute to savor the fabulousness of having Lily in my very own room. Then I tucked the shelter toys inside my nightstand. I knew those would be best used here, away from my mom, who was not going to be a fan of slightly gnawed playthings.

"Okay, let's go downstairs, get you fed, and get dinner started," I told Lily, who cheerfully bounded down the stairs after me.

In the kitchen I filled up her water dish, but Lily trailed after me until I got to the main event: a can of (organic) beef dog food that I ladled into her bowl. She wolfed it down and then dug into the scoop of kibble I served up next. Once she'd eaten she flopped down in front of the dishwasher looking content.

"I'm glad you liked it," I told her as I diced up potatoes just the way my mom had showed me. It was so nice having company as I started dinner!

A few minutes later the front door opened. Lily stood up and gave a short bark.

"That's my mom," I told her, wiping my hands quickly on a dish towel. "Come and meet her."

Lily and I walked into the living room where my mom was putting on her slippers. Lily barked again and my mom winced slightly.

"Here she is," I said proudly, petting Lily as I led her to my mom so that Lily would know my mom was a safe person. Not that Lily had ever been on guard with anyone, but animals had their own set of instincts and I knew Lily might behave slightly differently here, especially as she adjusted to the newness of it all.

But Lily had clearly already decided that she liked my mom because she padded right up to her, tail wagging, and leaned against my mom, opening her mouth in a doggy smile.

Unfortunately she caught my mom a bit off balance and nearly toppled her over. My mom righted herself before falling, but she was frowning as she looked down at her pants. "Well, these will need a wash, won't they," she said. "They're covered with dog hair."

"Mom, it's just a few pieces of hair," I said. "I'll get you the lint brush."

Lily, unaware of my mom's crabbiness, butted her head forward to be petted. She had really taken to my mom.

"No, they need to be cleaned," my mom said, patting Lily. Which was nice, though Lily hadn't given her much of a choice in the matter.

"Lily already ate," I said, starting back toward the kitchen. "And I started our dinner."

"Good," my mom said. Lily stayed right next to her

as we walked back to the kitchen.

"Sit," I told Lily, pointing to the spot near the dishwasher where Lily would be out of the way.

Lily sat, but not in her spot. Instead she sat right on my mom's feet, nearly tripping her. "I thought you said she was trained," my mom snapped.

"She is. She's just confused," I said.

I knew it was a mistake as soon as the words were out, but it was too late and my mom pounced on it. "Yes, older dogs like this confuse easily," she said.

"No, she was confused because my command wasn't clear," I said. I walked over to the spot and called Lily, who came right away. "See?" I asked.

My mom sniffed a bit, but couldn't deny that Lily was doing exactly what she had been told.

I was concerned that Lily might try to steal scraps under the table as we ate, but when she followed us into the dining room, I told her to sit and she did, right behind my chair. Every time I glanced back I could see her caramel-colored fur and sweet face looking at me. It was awesome, even if my mom did complain again about having to clean up dog fur.

After we washed up I headed into my mom's home office for the video chat with my dad. I couldn't wait for him to meet Lily! Well, really just see her, but that was a start.

"So where's our new foster dog?" my dad asked as soon as the screen flickered to life. I loved how exited he sounded.

I'd had Lily sit next to me while I waited and now I pushed my chair back and patted my lap. Lily jumped up and I wrapped my arms around her so she wouldn't slide off and peeked around her shaggy belly. "Meet Lily!" I nearly sang.

"Hi, Lily," my dad said with a huge smile.

Lily, hearing her name, barked back, as though she was greeting him, which made both of us laugh.

"She likes you already," I told my dad as I helped Lily off my lap so we'd be more comfortable. She sat close and rested her head on my leg as I continued to talk to my dad.

"I like her too," he said. He had dark circles under

his eyes, but they sparkled as he smiled again. "How does it feel to have her home?"

"It's so great," I said, and then proceeded to tell him everything. With Lily snuggling next to me and my dad nodding and asking all the right questions—and *not* saying anything about dog fur—it was the best.

The only thing better was getting into bed that night with Lily curling up right next to me, her soft head right at the crook of my arm.

"Good night, sweet girl," I said, turning off the light, my heart full as I nestled in closer to her and fell asleep.

9

Lily was gone in the morning. For a moment I worried the whole thing had been some kind of dream, but then I saw the nesting spot where she'd slept next to me all night. She was definitely here, but where? And what if she was doing something that might upset my mom? I leaped out of bed and rushed out of the room to find her.

She wasn't in the hall or the bathroom, and luckily she wasn't in my mom's empty bedroom either. I flew down the stairs and finally found Lily in the dining room with my mom, who was drinking her morning cup of coffee from her favorite butterfly mug.

"I'm already covered with dog hair," my mom announced, no "good morning" or anything as I came over and rubbed Lily's side.

My mom was petting Lily's head with the hand that wasn't gripping her coffee, which was great. But the way she was scowling was less great. A lot less great.

"How can one dog shed so much fur?" she groused, picking a piece off her pants.

"She has long hair," I said defensively. "And dogs shed when they're nervous. Lily's had a big change in her life and I think she's handling it great so far."

My mom shook her head dismissively. "The point is that she's barely groomed at all. I'm not sure anyone has ever taken the time to truly get her coat clean and shaped. She looks like a yeti."

A burst of anger crackled through me and I pressed my lips together to keep from saying something I'd regret. I wasn't even sure what a yeti was, but clearly it was bad and I hated hearing my mom criticize the club, not to mention the job I'd done brushing Lily the day before.

"I'm taking her to the Pampered Puppy," my mom announced. "If she's going to stay here for a few weeks she needs to look decent, and I can't spend the whole time cleaning up after her."

With that she headed upstairs to get ready for work, which was probably good because I was having trouble keeping my temper in check.

"You look perfect," I told Lily, hugging her close.

Lily licked my cheek, clearly unfazed by the fact that she had been insulted. Sometimes it was a good thing dogs couldn't always understand what people said.

I walked to the kitchen to see about feeding Lily, but when I got there I saw that my mom had already taken care of it. Which was probably why Lily was so calm, but it surprised me. We'd agreed that Lily's care would be my responsibility. For a moment I felt a flash of gratitude toward my mom, but then I realized Lily had probably been bouncing around in a way that was cute but that annoyed my mom. So my mom had probably fed her to calm her down. Which made it less nice.

"Let's go upstairs," I told Lily. "I'm going to get ready for school."

But just then my mom reappeared. "Lily, come," she called as she strode toward the front door.

I expected Lily to linger or at least look up at me, but she flew after my mom the second she heard her name. I couldn't believe how quickly she'd taken to my mom, even if the feeling wasn't completely mutual.

"She came right when you called," I pointed out as I followed them both to the front hall where my mom was putting on her shoes.

"I'd hope so," she sniffed, though I noticed her petting Lily between shoes.

I felt sad as I watched my mom leash Lily up. I was going to miss her as I got ready for school. But then I remembered she would be here when I got home and I got the happy fizzy bubbles in my stomach again.

"Have fun," I called to Lily as she and my mom headed out.

Lily gave a happy bark in response and pranced off after my mom.

I watched them for a moment and then headed back inside to get ready for the day.

"So how was your first night as a dog owner?" Taylor asked eagerly. She'd caught up to me just outside the cafeteria.

"Wait, I want to hear too," Kim said, coming up behind us. "And so will Sasha. Let's go sit and you can fill us in on everything."

"Okay," I agreed. It was exciting to be at the center of things as the three of them got food and we made our way over to our table. The main course today was beef stroganoff and the scent was overpowering. I was glad I'd brought lunch from home.

"Tell us," Taylor said, peeling off the foil lid of her yogurt after we'd all sat down.

"Yeah, how was it?" Emily asked as she, Naomi,

Dana, and Rachel crowded around.

"It was awesome," I said, my face suddenly warming. I wasn't used to this much attention from everyone. But they were all beaming, clearly thrilled for me, and that felt amazing. "Lily was so cute exploring everywhere and sniffing everything."

"Did she seem scared at all?" Emily asked. "When we brought my dog home from the shelter he hid behind the sofa for hours. We had to coax him out with food."

"No, she was pretty comfortable actually," I said, hoping that didn't hurt Emily's feelings. I wanted to be honest, but I also wanted to keep up with my promise to myself to be careful about what I said to people, and the way I said it.

"I think that's because you're familiar to her," Kim said knowledgably. "Em, your dog was facing new people and a new place, but Lily had her favorite person right there with her."

Kim always said the right thing.

"That makes sense," Emily said. "And he adapted

pretty fast after he figured out we gave food and treats on a regular basis."

We laughed at that as the four of them headed back to their table.

"I remember when Mr. S first came home," Sasha said, smiling at the memory. "For the first few weeks he had this ritual where he'd walk all over the house first thing in the morning, like he was making sure nothing had changed while he was sleeping."

"Remember how he carried that little pillow from your bedroom all over the place?" Taylor asked.

I had the fourth-wheel feeling as the three of them cracked up. I twisted the ponytail I'd curled that morning so hard it pulled my scalp.

"It was like his security blanket," Kim said. "Bri, does Lily have anything like that?"

"Not so far," I said, opening up my container of shredded potato and rice. "But she really liked the toys I brought home from the shelter." I'd let her play with them again before bed and she'd fallen asleep with the rubber hamburger in her mouth. I'd been careful to put it away before leaving for school.

"I'm glad," Kim said, taking a bite of her sandwich. "So what else did she do yesterday?"

We chowed down on our food as I told them about Lily's adventures.

"Did your mom totally fall in love with Lily?" Sasha asked after I described Lily "meeting" my dad.

My chest tightened up instantly. "Um, yeah, my mom was petting Lily a lot," I stammered, not wanting to lie but clearly not able to share the truth. "And she's taking Lily to the Pampered Puppy to groom her." I hadn't really wanted to tell them that either, but it was going to be obvious when they saw Lily.

"That's so nice," Taylor said. "It's like how a kid gets a haircut to look their best on the first day of school. Lily's getting a haircut to look her best in her new home."

And now it was Taylor who knew just the right thing to say.

"It sounds like it all went great," Kim said. She had

finished eating and was crumpling up her sandwich wrapper to recycle.

For a second I remembered my mom's scowl this morning, but I replaced it with the memory of snuggling down at night with Lily. "It really did," I said.

The next afternoon we had a quick stop to make before picking up our dogs. Marisol from Sugar and Spice had left a message for Sasha and we figured it made sense to get the news in person.

"I really hope they'll make the candy for us," Kim said as we hustled down Main Street. It was another windy day and leaves swirled around us.

"I know," Sasha agreed. "It would make our booth a real hot spot."

"And totally get out the word about our club and the foster program," I added as we came up to the little candy shop.

"Here goes," Taylor said, biting her lip the tiniest bit as she pulled open the door and the four of us walked inside.

Carmen was ringing up a customer, but she called Marisol in from the kitchen and a moment later she appeared, tray in hand. "Hello there, members of the Roxbury Park Dog Club," she said cheerfully. "Want to try some chocolate caramel bars?"

We were all eager to hear their decision, but no one was turning down that offer. We each took a little square. The chocolate was creamy in my mouth, and the caramel was so rich and sweet I nearly swooned.

"Those are amazing," I said when I'd finished mine.

"Totally," Taylor agreed.

"I'm so glad you think so," Marisol said, beaming. "Because this is the kind of candy we'll be donating to you guys for the craft fair!"

The four of us couldn't help cheering and Marisol laughed.

"When we realized the benefit of advertising our store along with such a great cause, there was no way we could turn you down," Carmen said, coming over to join us.

"We can shape them however you guys want," Marisol said. "We were thinking dog bones, but maybe you have another idea?"

Taylor glanced at me. "Actually, our program has a new logo," she said. "A paw print. Could we maybe get candy in the shape of a paw?"

Carmen nodded. "That's easy enough," she said. "And we can print the logo on the foil wrapper, along with your contact info and a tagline about our store."

"Perfect," Kim said with a grin.

It really was.

Lily was beside herself when we walked into the shelter for Dog Club. She was already pretty amped up after the fun of going to Waffles's and then Coco's house to pick them up. But being back with all her friends, in the place she'd lived for years, had her racing in wild circles.

"Someone's happy to see friends," Alice said, laughing as Lily actually jumped up on hind legs to give Alice a kiss.

Lily wasn't the only one who was happy. Alice squeezed her extra tight as the other dogs crowded around her, and Tim and Caley rushed over to hug her. Kim, Sasha, and Taylor, who had arrived before us, were right behind.

But as soon as she had greeted everyone, Lily came right over to me, sat at my feet, and looked up as if to say, "Did you see all that?"

"Aw, she loves you so much," Taylor said. Jinx was leaning against her legs and Taylor was rubbing the back of her neck with her knuckles.

"She does," Kim agreed from the floor where she'd settled to snuggle with Boxer.

Alice nodded. "Looks like you and Lily are a perfect fit."

We really were. And if everyone else could see it, my mom had to as well. As I hugged Lily close, then released her to play with her friends, I vowed to stay patient with my mom and do everything I could to show her that Lily was meant to stay with us, forever.

"She sure looks snazzy," Caley said, observing Lily's

sleekness after her time at the Pampered Puppy. Her fur was extra fluffy and neatly shaped and trimmed.

"How nice that your mom took her to get washed and have a haircut," Alice said.

"Yeah, she was excited to do it," I said somewhat awkwardly. My mom *had* been excited of course, but for the wrong reasons.

"So the craft fair is in twelve days," Alice said, thankfully changing the subject from my mom. Missy pressed against her leg and Alice crouched down to pet her. "And I think we're in great shape. You guys did an awesome job getting the Lopez sisters to donate candy for us to sell." Sasha had texted Alice the good news as soon as we'd found out. "We need to choose pictures and make the layout for the calendar. And then I think we should come up with one more item to sell."

"I can still make that video of Coach Tim's doggy basketball tips," Tim offered from across the room where he was playing fetch with Lily, Gus, Mr. S, Popsicle, Gracie, and Coco.

"We were hoping you'd offer," Caley teased with

an eye roll. She was tossing a tennis ball for Daisy, Waffles, and Hattie.

Tim gave her a mock sour look and then was nearly barreled over by Boxer, who had decided to join the game.

"Maybe we should print our own T-shirts," Kim said. She'd gotten up and was encouraging Humphrey to chase the blue rubber bone. Humphrey clearly enjoyed sniffing it, but looked at Kim skeptically when she threw it a few feet away. After a moment he padded after it. "We could put Bri's logo on them."

"A lot of places will sell T-shirts, though," Taylor said. "I think we should come up with something more creative."

"A video would be very creative and—hey!" Tim howled, cut off by Caley socking him good-naturedly on the arm.

"Enough with the video," she told him.

"Well, that's just rude," Tim joked, making us giggle.

"What about some other kind of clothing, like socks?" Kim asked.

"Socks would be cute, but I'm not sure we could just order them from Lester's," Sasha said.

Both Taylor and I looked at her, confused. It was nice to not be the fourth wheel for once.

"Who's Lester?" Taylor asked. Waffles had wandered over and Taylor was rubbing her ears gently.

Kim smiled. "That's the shop that prints up stuff like T-shirts for local businesses and fund-raisers and sports teams," she said. "It's just off Main Street."

"They do simple things like shirts and banners, but socks might be a bit much," Sasha said. "Plus it's not good advertising because no one goes around reading other people's socks."

I snickered. "It would be funny if they did though."

Everyone laughed at that.

"Let's keep thinking about it," Alice said, standing up. "I need to pack up the empty bags and boxes for the recycling pick up later this afternoon."

"Oh, that gives me an idea," Sasha squealed. "What if we made up special reusable bags, the cloth or canvas kind people bring to the grocery store so they don't waste a plastic bag?"

"My dad totally uses those," Taylor said, sounding enthused.

"My parents too," Kim said. "I think a lot of people do."

"Yeah, we have some," I said, thinking of the neat stack of bags my mom pulled out each time she shopped for food.

"I love that idea," Alice agreed.

"And it's a nice big space to put our logo and all our info," Sasha said with satisfaction.

"We could put our logo on one side and something else fun on the other side," I said, getting excited as I thought about all the design potential on a whole big bag. Lily heard my cheeriness and came over for a quick hug. I was so happy she'd be coming home with me that night.

"That would be great," Taylor agreed. "What could we put on the other side?"

I thought about it for a moment as I picked up a ball to play with Lily and Coco, who had come over too. "What about something simple, like a black and white silhouette of a person and a dog, maybe walking together?"

Taylor clapped her hands. "Love it!" she proclaimed.

"Me too," Kim agreed. "The only thing is that bags might be expensive."

It was a good point. I could tell everyone else agreed because we were all silent for a moment, with just the sounds of barks, yips, and running dogs filling the air.

But then Sasha spoke up. "I wonder if my mom might want to sponsor the bags," she said thought-fully. "The way Carmen and Marisol are sponsoring the candy."

"I bet she'd totally want to do that," Taylor said. "It would be great advertising for the law firm, since they specialize in environmental law and reusable bags help the environment."

"And your mom always loves to support the Dog Club," Kim added from the corner where she was now playing tug-of-war with Hattie. I felt a flash of jealousy at how all the other parents supported the club while my mom just insulted it.

"I'll ask her tonight," Sasha declared. "But I'm sure she'll say yes. And Bri, when she does, will you draw up that silhouette?"

"Sure, I'd be happy to," I said, pleased to be asked.

"So we have a plan," Alice said. "And I like it."

She headed back to the office while Kim and Sasha began to organize a trip to the backyard. For a moment I worried that Lily would get dirty running around out there, but I shrugged it off. There'd be time to clean her, and Lily loved a good romp in the sun.

So the two of us headed out with everyone else, ready for an afternoon of fun.

10

Lily and I were a bit late getting home that night. It had taken me a while to clean her off after she and Boxer had landed in a mud puddle while chasing the ball in doggy tag. And unfortunately my mom was already home when we arrived.

"Hi, Mom," I called, nearly tripping as I rushed to get my shoes off. "Sorry we're late."

My mom was frowning when Lily and I got into

the kitchen. "We agreed that your chores wouldn't suffer if that dog came to live with us," my mom said.

My back stiffened up at the way she didn't even say Lily's name. But I remembered my vow to be patient and took a deep breath before answering. "I'm really sorry I wasn't here to start dinner," I said, going to the sink to wash my hands. "But it won't happen again and I can help now."

"I already did most of it," my mom said. "But you can slice the garlic and ginger."

"Okay," I said, grabbing a cutting board.

I noticed Lily walk over to my mom and press against her legs. I worried my mom would snap at Lily the way she was snapping at me, but instead she just patted Lily's head. "You can feed her first," my mom said. "That way she won't be underfoot."

Lily danced around me as I served up her dinner and then stayed in her section of the kitchen while my mom and I finished preparing dinner.

"I brought you something," my mom said, after

we'd sat down and started eating. She passed me a bro-chure.

I looked down at the pictures of poodles, cocker spaniels, and Irish setters. "Puppy Rescue," the title said. Just like that my appetite was gone.

"We have Lily," I said, pushing the pamphlet back toward my mom.

"Yes, but that's temporary," my mom said briskly. "I want us to start thinking about a permanent situation with a dog who could stay with us forever. A dog we rescue, who really needs a home."

How could she not see that that dog was Lily?

"Puppies are so cute and they learn fast," my mom said, opening up to a picture of a dachshund doing some kind of elaborate rolling over trick. "A dog like that will be a better fit for our home."

"Lily learns fast," I said, pushing my garlic beef and rice around on my plate. "And she's really sweet."

My mom sniffed dismissively and waved her hand. "She does her best, but she has bad habits from that shelter and because of her age she's clearly limited in the skills she's able to master."

Now I was gritting my teeth.

"Let me give you an example," my mom said, and then told a long story about Franz from the Pampered Puppy, who had learned to sit, stay, and fetch on his very first day. "See, that's the thing about younger dogs who haven't already developed bad habits," my mom said, scraping up the last bite from her plate. "You know exactly what you're getting when you adopt one. With a dog like this," she said, gesturing toward Lily, who was now next to my mom, "it's an uphill battle." My mom patted Lily on the head and Lily, having no idea she was being insulted, leaned affectionately against her leg.

"Lily knows how to sit and stay and fetch, though," I pointed out. "So even if she's slow to train, she's got those skills now."

"Right, but what happens when we want to teach her a new skill to help her fit into our home?" my mom asked, raising an eyebrow. "For example, not coming up to the table while people are eating?"

"But you just pet her," I said, anger heating up my belly. "You reinforced the behavior."

My mom looked surprised for a moment, then glanced down to where Lily now had her head resting against my mom's knee. And where my mom was still petting her. "Well, she's not here very long," my mom said defensively. "And I was done eating. The point is, she doesn't have very good manners and who knows how long it would take to retrain her."

"It could be—" I began, but my mom cut me off.

"The bottom line is that we're lucky we don't need to find out because Lily's just a foster," she said, standing up. "In a few weeks she'll be someone else's problem."

It was a good thing she started clearing her place, because it was taking everything in me not to snap at her. I couldn't believe she'd call Lily a problem, especially when Lily pranced happily next to her as she went to the kitchen.

I stood up to clear my half-eaten dinner. I wanted to go upstairs and start making my design for the reusable bag, since Sasha's mom would most likely agree to it. Unlike my mom, the other parents actually supported our club.

But just then I heard my phone beep with a text. Normally it was up in my room during dinner. My mom had a strict no-phones-near-dinner rule. But I'd been in such a rush earlier that my backpack was still in the front hall, and I went over now to see who had texted.

"Can u host slpovr this wkend?" It was from Taylor. "We all wnt to hang w/ Lily."

I bit my lip as I stared at the screen. There was no way they could come here. My mom would complain about Lily and then insult the shelter. And she'd probably manage to do all of it before my friends had even made it inside the house.

"Srry cnt this time," I typed in, adding a sad emoji. I'd tell them that my mom was doing a weekend cleanup at the Pampered Puppy. Or that she was feeling under the weather.

But I knew that sooner or later my excuses would run out, and then what?

"So I narrowed it down to twenty potential calendar shots," Taylor said at lunch, taking a folder out of her bag. The cafeteria smelled of overcooked broccoli and the gray day outside matched my mood. But the thought of selecting the pictures for our Dogs at Play calendar cheered me up and I dug into my leftover beef and rice.

"I remember this," Sasha said, picking up a picture of Mr. S and Hattie touching noses. Hattie was small in the photo—she'd been a puppy when she first arrived at the shelter though she'd grown a lot—so it was obviously from before I'd joined the club.

"Hattie was so shy," Taylor reminisced. "But you really brought her out of her shell," she added, nodding to Kim, whose cheeks turned pink.

"I think we all helped Hattie," she said.

Though of course that "all" didn't include me since I hadn't even been there. My gloomy mood was starting to seep back.

"Here's a doggy basketball shot, for Tim," Taylor said, passing me a gorgeous picture of Popsicle dunking the ball.

"Let's use that one for January," I said, happy to be back in the conversation.

"Sounds good," Taylor said as Kim and Sasha nodded. "One down, eleven more to go."

"So which dogs did you choose for the calendar?" Caley asked at the next club meeting. She was playing fetch with Lily, Boxer, and Gus while Tim and I got things ready for a game of doggy basketball. Hattie, Daisy, Jinx, Gracie, Tuesday, and Mr. S were "helping" us by stealing the ball and jumping into the basket whenever we tried to move it, so it was taking a while.

"I'll show you," Taylor said, pulling out her phone and scrolling through photos. She was with Humphrey and Missy, who lazed happily at her feet.

"Tim, you're going to like it," I promised as he and Caley headed to Taylor to check out the shot.

Tim cheered when he saw it. "A doggy basketball action shot," he said. "The best way to kick off the year."

"Show us the rest," Caley said eagerly. She cooed over February's photo of Boxer leaping for his Frisbee and the March group scene of five of our dogs chasing a tennis ball across the big main room.

"We should be sure to talk to dog owners today, to get their okay on putting their dogs in the calendar," Alice said. She'd come out of her office to see the pictures too. "And then I'll email everything to Lester's."

"I already printed up a release," Sasha said, taking a stack of papers from her backpack. "My mom helped me."

"It's always good to have a lawyer in the family," Alice said with a grin. Then she turned to me. "Bri, do you have a minute?"

"Sure," I said, following her into her office and hoping nothing was wrong. I sat down and tucked a few stray strands of hair back into the twisty bun I'd sculpted this morning. Even with a lot of hairspray some bits were escaping.

"I just wanted to check in and see how everything's going with Lily," Alice said, settling into the chair behind her desk. "I can see how happy she is when she comes in for the club, but I wanted to make sure everything is smooth at home, too."

"Um, yeah, it's good," I said, fumbling a little. I didn't want to lie to Alice, but there was no way I was admitting the things my mom said. "Lily is really comfortable and I love having her." That was true. "And Lily likes my mom a lot." That was also, mysteriously, true. Though of course my mom was kind to Lily. I always saw her petting Lily in the morning when I came down for breakfast, and last night I'd caught her cooing to Lily over a toy Lily had dropped at her feet.

"I'm so glad to hear it," Alice said. "And I think that means I can start the process of taking in a dog from one of the shelters, to take Lily's place."

"That's great," I said. I loved the idea of saving one of those dogs that would otherwise be put down.

Despite my mom's bad attitude, I was proud we'd taken in a foster dog so that another dog could have a second chance to find a home.

"The process will take a week or two," Alice said. "And my hope is that after the craft fair we'll have more offers for fostering and more spots opening up."

"That would be awesome," I said, happy at the thought of lots of dogs finding homes instead of being put to sleep.

"Keep me posted if anything changes with Lily," Alice said, standing up.

"I will," I said, heading out. My fingers were crossed that the change would be from us fostering Lily to adopting her, but so far there was no sign of that happening.

Still, as the game of doggy basketball began, with Lily, Gracie, Daisy, and Coco making mad dashes for the basket while Waffles and Popsicle tried to steal the ball and stuff it back in the toy bin, I let myself picture how perfect it would be if Lily was mine forever.

11

"Is Lily ready for her doggy sleepover?" Sasha asked, opening up the door to her house. Taylor, Kim, and Mr. S stood right behind her, and Lily, who I'd brought with me, barked in happy greeting.

"She sure is," I said with a smile as I let her off her leash.

When I couldn't host, Sasha came up with the idea of a double sleepover: one for us humans and one for Lily and Mr. S.

Lily rushed inside where she and Mr. S sniffed in greeting and then began romping together.

"This is too cute," Sasha squealed.

Taylor had her camera out and was taking pictures. "This is seriously the sweetest thing ever."

Kim was grinning as she watched the dogs play. "I can't wait 'til tonight when they realize Lily's staying. I bet they'll curl up in the same dog bed together."

I would miss Lily cuddling next to me at night, but it would be worth it to see her and Mr. S all tucked in together.

Sasha led the way up to her room. Lily stopped to inspect everything along the way and Mr. S stood beside her, ever the good host. I put my backpack and sleeping bag on the floor in the corner, where Kim and Taylor had already piled their things.

"I wanted to wait until everyone got here to tell you the good news," Sasha said, sitting down on her bed and bouncing a bit as she spoke. "My mom loved the idea of the reusable bags! Her firm will totally sponsor them."

"Awesome," Taylor said happily, sitting down next to Sasha.

"Totally," Kim agreed. She perched on Sasha's desk chair while I sat down on the floor where I could cuddle the dogs.

"So Bri, whenever you're ready you can make the design for the back of the bag," Sasha said. "I called Lester's and they said if we get everything to them by Monday the bags will be ready for the craft festival."

"Actually," I said sheepishly, "I already started. I have a design I like and I brought it with me if you guys want to check it out."

"Of course!" Taylor said.

I grabbed my backpack and pulled a folder out of it. "I tried out a couple of things," I said. "And I think this one is the best. But if you guys don't like it I can definitely make another." It was a silhouette of a kid and a dog, standing under a tree. The dog was standing on her hind paws, with her front paws on the shoulders of the kid. And I'd angled the dog's head so that you could

144

tell she was giving her owner a big kiss.

I passed it over to Taylor while Kim and Sasha came to peer at it from either side.

"It's wonderful," Kim said, almost breathlessly. "Bri, you are seriously talented."

I ducked my head as my cheeks heated up. It still felt strange to be sharing my artwork, but my friends' support made it a lot easier.

"I love it too," Sasha exclaimed, jumping up. "Let's go show my mom right now."

So back downstairs we went, the dogs right behind us. Sasha's mom was in the kitchen, cell phone pressed to her ear. She was grinning broadly at whatever the person on the other end was saying, and after a moment she let out a peal of laughter.

The dogs raced over and she bent down to rub Mr. S's ears and let Lily sniff her hand in greeting. "The girls and the dogs are here so I need go," she said into the phone. Then she hung up, her eyes still bright. "Taylor, that was your dad and he said hi," she said. "And reminded you not to drink too many milk shakes."

We all laughed at that. Mr. S went over to his water dish, but Lily stayed next to Sasha's mom, who stroked the soft fur on Lily's chest. "Aren't you a beauty," she cooed to Lily.

I couldn't help feeling jealous that Sasha's mom was so great about Lily. But I was also happy for Sasha, since I knew it had taken a lot of coaxing to turn her mom into a dog owner willing to host a doggy sleepover.

"We have something to show you," Sasha bubbled. "It's the picture Bri made for the reusable bag."

"Ooh, let's see," Sasha's mom said, standing up.

Sasha handed her the paper and I realized my heart was banging in my chest as her mother stared down at it. What if she hated it?

After a moment she looked up at me, her face serious. "Bri, you are quite talented," she said. "You could have a real future in graphic design if you chose to."

For the second time in ten minutes my face warmed.

"It's perfect, right?" Sasha asked. "And the logo and

all our information and the tag from your firm will go in the other side."

"Sounds like a plan," her mom said. "I can take everything to Lester's if you guys want."

I kind of wanted to take it myself, to talk to Lester about layout, but Sasha was already nodding. "That would be great, thanks," she said.

"Yes, it's a big help," Kim agreed. "Thanks."

I was disappointed not to get to go to the store, but clearly no one else felt that way so I kept it to myself.

"Dinner is almost ready if you ladies want to set the table," Sasha's mom said. "I slaved over it all day, so I hope you like it."

I was ready to thank her, but everyone else burst out laughing.

"I just ordered pizza," Sasha's mom said when she noticed my confusion. "The others know that's what we usually do when Sasha hosts."

Of course they all knew. And of course I didn't since I'd only been to a few sleepovers.

"We always get mushroom and pepperoni," Sasha added.

"It's our favorite combo," Taylor added, but then she looked at me. "That's okay, right?"

Actually, I hated mushrooms. But I didn't want to be any more of a fourth wheel than I already was. "Sure," I lied, pasting a smile on my face. "That sounds great."

"Hi, Mom, we're home," I called as Lily and I walked into the house on Sunday afternoon.

My mom walked in, pulling the vacuum behind her. Her mouth was pursed. "I finally got the house clean and here she is, ready to shed all over it again," she complained, glaring at Lily.

I was tired from lack of sleep and still crabby from feeling left out. In other words, I was in no mood for another one of my mom's anti-Lily rants.

"I'm going to take a nap," I said. I always napped after sleepovers since we were up half the night.

"I was hoping you'd offer to help me clean, but I suppose that's too much to ask," my mom said.

"But you told me you just cleaned," I exclaimed, throwing up my hands.

"I meant after that dog messes up the house again," my mom snapped as Lily bounded upstairs.

I closed my eyes, the start of a headache tapping at my temples. "Mom, her name is Lily, not 'that dog,'" I said, trying not to snap back.

"Well, she's just here a few more weeks," my mom said grimly, her words slicing into me just as Lily pranced back into the room, the chewed up plastic hamburger in her mouth. She headed right for my mom and dropped the toy at my mom's feet, then wagged her tail, ready to play fetch.

"What is that?" my mom gasped, recoiling as though Lily had dropped a dead snake at her feet. "And where did it come from?"

"It's one of Lily's toys from the shelter," I said, annoyed with myself that I hadn't made sure to lock it up. "I think it made her feel comfortable when she first got here."

"I should have known," my mom said darkly. "Of course the shelter allows animals to play with mangled-up toys that probably contain lead paint."

"Mom, it's not poisoned," I said sharply, scooping up the hamburger. Lily, thinking I planned to throw it for her to fetch, began to bark happily.

"Lily, quiet!" my mom said, scowling.

But that was not a command Lily knew, so she kept barking.

"You don't train dogs, you give them unsafe toys," my mom began.

"Mom, stop," I shouted, fed up. "You have no idea what the shelter is like because you've never even been there."

My tone scared Lily, who cowered in the corner. I hated that I'd upset her, but I was so angry at my mom that I was shaking. "You don't care what I want," I went on. "I love the shelter, I love Lily, but all you do is put down both of them."

"I think that's overstating it a bit," my mom sniffed, like I was totally overreacting.

Which made my anger turn into rage, the kind where I didn't think, I just let the words pour out. "Fine," I fumed. "If you don't want Lily, I don't want her either. We can return her to the shelter tomorrow."

There was a short silence as we both absorbed what I'd said. I opened my mouth, wanting to take it back, but my mom spoke first.

"I'm glad you suggested it," she said. "It's the right thing to do. I have my hands full enough as it is with your dad away so much. We need a dog that's trainable, who can learn to fit in with our family, not one that creates this much work. I'll drop her off first thing in the morning."

My eyes filled with tears as I stared at Lily, my heart breaking, but the damage was already done.

12

"See you guys at the shelter," Kim said. It was after school the next day and we were splitting up to get our dogs for the club meeting. I'd put off telling my friends what had happened with Lily, but I knew I had to say something now. It would just be harder if I waited until the shelter, when Lily would be there.

"I, uh, have something to tell you," I said, then cleared my throat. It was going to take everything in me to get the words out without totally bawling. "My mom and I decided we needed to stop fostering Lily."

Sasha gasped, Kim's eyes widened, and Taylor reached out and grabbed my arm. "What happened?" she asked.

"I guess it was just a little too much for my mom," I said, my voice squeaky. "Lily sheds a lot and her training is really different from dogs at the Pampered Puppy." I took a shaky breath. "I feel really bad letting Alice and everyone down but—"

"Don't worry about that," Taylor said firmly, wrapping an arm around my shoulder. It felt good.

"Taylor's right," Kim agreed. "If it wasn't working, the best thing was to take Lily back."

"We're just sorry because we know how much you love Lily," Sasha said sympathetically.

Now I was blinking back tears. "We should probably go pick up the club dogs now," I said, tugging on a lock of hair. I hadn't bothered to put it up this morning. Nothing, not even a fun hairstyle, was going to cheer me up today.

"Is there anything we can do?" Taylor asked.

I shook my head. "No," I said. "But thanks for asking."

Lily bounded up to me the second I walked into the shelter with Humphrey, Popsicle, and Mr. S. As soon as I'd let them off their leashes I bent down and hugged her close, burying my face in her soft fur. She barked happily, probably thinking she was coming home with me after the meeting, like always. The thought made my chest ache.

"Hi, Bri," Alice said. "Let's talk when you're ready."

I took a deep breath and followed her into her office. "I'm sorry," I said, before even sitting down. "I know you were getting another dog and I know you were counting on us to keep Lily and—"

Alice held up a hand and I stopped talking and sank into the chair across from her desk.

"It's okay, Bri," Alice said, her voice kind. "These things happen. If it wasn't the right fit then it's best for Lily to be back here."

It was just what Kim had said, but it didn't make me feel better. "Lily was the perfect fit for me," I mumbled.

Alice reached out and took one of my hands. "I'm sorry it didn't work out," she said, her gentle tone bringing me dangerously close to tears.

"Thanks," I said, when I could speak clearly.

"We'll take good care of her here," Alice assured me. "And you'll see her every time you come in for Dog Club."

It wasn't the same but I nodded, appreciating how nice Alice was being. I knew it was hard for her that we'd returned Lily, especially after I'd told her last week that everything was fine.

I headed out to the big room where Gracie, Gus, Waffles, Coco, and Mr. S were playing fetch with Caley. Tim was wrestling with Boxer, Lily, Daisy, Jinx, Tuesday, and Hattie. Popsicle and Missy were chasing a tennis ball and Humphrey was napping in the corner, next to Kim, Taylor, and Sasha, who were standing in a tight circle and speaking in low voices. The minute Taylor caught sight of me she cleared her throat and the three of them looked at me almost guiltily. Great, I was the fourth wheel again, on what was already one of the worst days of my life.

"Lester's called," Sasha said brightly as she picked up the tennis ball to throw for Missy and Popsicle. "The bags and calendars will be ready on Friday and my mom said she'll pick them up after work."

"And the Lopezes emailed to say that the chocolates are all ready and they'll bring them to the booth on Saturday," Kim said.

I'd almost forgotten that the craft festival was this weekend. At least that would help find foster families so we could still save that dog who was supposed to take Lily's place at the shelter.

"Perfect," Taylor said, grabbing the blue rubber bone to play with Coco, who had wandered over.

Boxer came up to me, his Frisbee in his mouth. I sent it flying across the room and he raced after it, Lily on his heels. It hurt to look at her, knowing she would never be mine, so I went over to Humphrey and began rubbing his belly. He sighed contentedly.

"I was thinking that maybe we should have a couple of the dogs hang out with us at the booth during the festival," Kim said. "So people can see how sweet and friendly they are."

"Great idea," Alice said. She was getting ready to go to the bank but stopped to pet Oscar in his bed on the windowsill. "I think we could do each dog for two hours at a time so they don't get overtired."

Kim was nodding. "That sounds good."

"People won't be able to resist signing up, or at least donating money, when they meet some of these sweeties," Caley said. She was cuddling Jinx, who licked her cheek, as though agreeing.

"Why don't you guys come up with a schedule?" Alice asked.

"We're on it," Taylor said.

Alice headed out and Taylor got out her phone to record our list.

"Boxer might have trouble sitting too long," Kim

said, looking around the room. "But I think Tuesday would be perfect."

"So she can take the first slot," Taylor said, typing it into her phone. "From ten to twelve."

I cleared my throat. "Lily would be great too."

Taylor shot me a sympathetic look. "Are you sure?"

I nodded mechanically. It wasn't what I wanted, but it was best for Lily and that mattered more. "I know she'd be happy if another family could take her in."

"What—" Tim began, but Kim shot him a look and he closed his mouth. Which I really appreciated, because there was no way I could tell the story of our failed foster experience again without bursting into tears.

"Lily from twelve to two, and then how about Gracie from two to four?" Sasha said.

"Perfect," Taylor said, typing it and then sliding her phone into her pocket. "I'll show Alice the list when she gets back."

"And one of us can be in charge of walking each

dog to and from the shelter," Kim said.

"I think we have everything set for the festival," Caley said.

"Well, then you know what that means," Tim said.

"What?" Caley asked.

"It's time for a game of doggy tag!"

So we all headed outside into the sunny afternoon to play with the dogs.

I'd done my best to stay cheerful, but by the time the last club dog had been picked up, all I wanted was to climb into bed and pull the covers over my head, possibly forever.

Lily bounded up to me when she saw me putting on my coat, but Alice quickly took Lily into her office. I wanted to thank Alice, but the lump in my throat made it impossible to say anything. So I waved quickly and ducked out, then headed home alone, my feet heavy and my heart aching with every step.

13

The next morning when I woke up, my first thought was to run downstairs and see Lily, who would be having morning coffee with my mom. But then the truth hit me like a ton of bricks and I rolled over and closed my eyes. Last night had been awful. My mom was falsely cheerful at a dinner that I could barely choke down. I saw her glance toward the spot where Lily usually sat, but then she just made a remark about the house being clean and left it at that.

The house may have been clean, but it was also unbearably empty. I missed Lily when I cleaned up after we'd eaten, when I went upstairs to do my homework, and most of all when I went to sleep, the bed cold without Lily curled next to me.

And I missed her now, the emptiness squeezing my chest and throat, making it hard to breathe.

It was quiet when I finally dragged myself downstairs. I made a piece of toast and went in to sit with my mom in the dining room as she drank her coffee. I noticed her eyes drifting over to Lily's spot and it suddenly occurred to me that maybe she missed Lily too. But then she cleared her throat.

"Bun, when you're ready, let's look this over and decide what kind of dog we want to get," my mom said, passing me a brochure from Puppy Rescue. She must have gotten a bunch, because I'd tossed the last one in the recycling bin.

"I know you miss that dog, but we did the right thing," my mom went on. "She was untrained and messy and she wasn't a good fit for our family. It was smart to cut it off now, since it clearly wasn't working."

"It was working for me," I said.

My mom glanced toward Lily's spot again and for a moment a look of sadness seemed to flash across her face. But then she straightened her shoulders.

"What's done is done," she said, and then she headed out.

After she'd gone I gathered my stuff for school. But before I left I made sure to throw the brochure into recycling.

Because if I couldn't have Lily, I didn't want a dog at all.

When I went to our regular meeting spot on the walk to school, I saw that Kim, Taylor, and Sasha had arrived before me, and once again they were in a tight circle speaking in low voices. And once again they stopped the second they saw me. The same thing happened at lunch. So I probably shouldn't have been surprised that they weren't even waiting for me at the end of the day. We didn't have Dog Club, but we still usually walked out together. But today they'd clearly ditched me and I had a feeling I knew why: Lily.

I walked slowly down the hall filled with groups of friends talking and laughing together. I got stuck behind a crowd of eighth-grade girls shrieking about a video one of them had made, but it wasn't like I was in a rush to get anywhere. I certainly wasn't going to go to the Pampered Puppy.

I finally made it out into the cloudy afternoon and couldn't help looking to see if maybe my friends had waited for me out here. But while the path outside school was filled with students, none of them was Kim, Sasha, or even Taylor. Not that I had expected them, of course.

Sure my friends had been sympathetic, but taking Lily and then returning her to the shelter was hard for a dog. That and the fact that I'd let down Alice and a dog that desperately needed a home—well, who could blame my friends for being annoyed about it? And there was no way to make them understand what really happened and how hard I'd fought for Lily. Not without spilling the truth about my mom. And the fact that my friends were ditching me now confirmed that I had been right not to trust them with that.

My phone vibrated with a text and I pulled it out.

"Come to the Rox." It was from Taylor.

Maybe my friends hadn't blown me off after all. Or were they going to tell me all the ways they were upset with me while we ate an after-school snack? I reminded myself that even if they were mad, they weren't mean, and they wouldn't try to make me feel bad. At least not on purpose. But my stomach was in knots when I pulled open the door to the cozy diner, the smells of fresh apple pie, coffee, and sweet potato fries, the house specialty, making me slightly queasy.

But when I saw my friends crowded into a booth, their faces lighting up when they saw me, I knew I'd gotten it wrong. This was not a bash-Bri event.

"We wanted to do something to cheer you up," Taylor said, bouncing up to give me a hug.

"We know how sad you are about Lily," Sasha said compassionately.

"Not that this makes up for losing her or anything," Kim said as I slid onto the vinyl cushioned bench across from her. They'd ordered drinks and I saw that they'd remembered my favorite was strawberry lemonade. They'd gotten me a large.

"But we figured snacks and a good talk were better than nothing," Taylor finished. "Sweet potato fries and cupcakes are on the way."

I realized that she was missing her photography class and that Sasha was skipping dance. And Kim was supposed to be with Anna. But instead they were here with me, hoping to cheer me up. I felt awful that I'd doubted them. And the only way to fix that was to come clean.

"You guys are the best," I said. "When I saw you talking before I thought you were mad at me."

Sasha's forehead wrinkled into a frown. "Why

would we be mad at you?" she asked.

"Because I let everybody down, even Lily," I said, my voice breaking.

"Oh, Bri, you didn't let us down," Taylor cried.

"We know this was harder on you than anyone," Sasha said, taking paper off her straw and putting it in her iced tea. "And we totally get that sometimes parents and kids don't see eye to eye on things."

I knew I could have left it at that, my friends understanding and accepting what I'd told them. But now that I'd seen how much they cared about me, and how they had my back no matter what, I knew I owed them better. More than that, I knew I could trust them with the truth—the whole truth.

"I haven't exactly told you everything," I said, running my finger through the film of condensation on the side of my glass.

My friends looked at me, waiting but not judging. I could see that now that I was really looking.

So I took a deep breath. "It's my mom," I said. "She

doesn't like our Dog Club. At all. She thinks the shelter takes in too many older dogs, she doesn't think we train them well, and she thinks the shelter is one big disaster zone."

It felt so good to finally admit this out loud.

"Wow," Taylor said, sitting back in the booth. "That's a lot."

The corners of Sasha's mouth were turning down. "She told you all this?"

I nodded.

Taylor reached out and patted my hand. "That must have really hurt your feelings."

Once again my eyes pricked with tears because I'd never thought about it quite like that before. I knew it made me mad, but Taylor was right: my mom's remarks didn't just anger me, they hurt me. "It really does," I said with a gulp.

Kim's brows scrunched together. "Have you ever told your mom how she makes you feel?"

"Um, actually, I just get angry and say mean stuff

back," I said, sending a guilty look toward Taylor. She knew how I could be when I got upset and didn't think before letting the words fly out.

But Taylor just laughed. "Oh, Bri, you need anger management."

That cracked me up and the others began laughing once I did.

"You might be right," I said, taking a long sip of my strawberry lemonade, the tangy sweetness soothing me.

"But it sounds like your mom needs it even more," Kim said with a frown. "She shouldn't say stuff that makes you feel bad."

"Maybe she doesn't know how much it upsets you," Sasha added.

Just then two baskets piled high with crispy spiced sweet potato fries arrived at the table. "Eat up," Kim's mom said with a smile before heading back to the kitchen.

I realized I was starving and I also wanted to think for a second about what my friends were saying. Because it was very possible that they were right.

"Sometimes parents need things explained," Kim said after we'd inhaled half of the first basket and were ready to talk again. "Remember when my parents thought I'd be better off at private school?"

Finally a memory that I was part of. Though it made me shudder. It would have been awful if we'd lost Kim.

"And it took forever to get my mom to agree to a dog," Sasha said.

"And you guys know how Anna and I misunderstood each other for ages," Taylor added. "Bri, it sounds like maybe that's kind of what's happening with you and your mom."

Maybe it was. I chewed a fry as I considered it.

"You know, I was kidding before about you needing anger management," Taylor said. "Because honestly, Bri, you are being so much more thoughtful. Like I can see you taking a minute to think before you say stuff and you never did that before."

"Yeah, I've been working on that," I said, pleased she'd noticed.

"So maybe your mom can learn to do the same

169

thing," Sasha said. "Like my mom learned to live with a little dog hair."

"I'm not sure," I said. Would my mom really be willing to change?

"You should give it a try," Kim encouraged me. "The worst thing that happens is that nothing changes."

"And you'll know you did your best," Taylor said. "That's always worth something. Though I do think your mom will feel bad she's upset you so much."

Something occurred to me. "You guys have never even met her," I teased. "She could be the Wicked Witch of the West."

"Impossible," Taylor said, shaking a fry at me. "No one who cooks Chinese food as amazing as your mom's is anything but a good witch."

"She just wears a Pampered Puppy coat instead of a pink gown," Sasha said with a giggle.

"It's the fashionable look for today's good witch," Taylor said in a mock haughty voice. But then she looked at me seriously. "You should trust your mom enough to tell her your true feelings."

She was right. And there were three other people I now knew I could trust with my real feelings, too.

"Thanks, you guys," I said. "I'll give it a try. And I have another confession."

"Well, wait for the cupcakes," Taylor said, feigning dismay. "Otherwise you'll overwhelm us."

Sasha laughed as she poked Taylor. "Go ahead, Bri," she told me.

"Sometimes I feel left out when the four of us are together," I said in a small voice, swishing my straw in the dregs of my lemonade. "You guys have so many memories together and traditions and favorite pizzas. I'm like the fourth wheel."

Taylor frowned slightly. "Isn't a fourth wheel a good thing? That's what balances out the car. Or truck or whatever vehicle we are."

I laughed a little at that. "Yeah, it doesn't really make sense, but that's how I think about it, like the three of you fit together and I'm kind of this add-on."

Sasha tilted her head slightly. "You are a bit of a fourth wheel, Bri," she said. "But the good kind, like Taylor was talking about. You're the part we were missing."

"I agree," Kim said. "You give our group fire and passion."

"You're honest and tell it like it is," Sasha added. "In a good way."

"You come up with awesome ideas," Taylor said. "And your designs are amazing."

"Yeah, we'd be lost without you," Sasha said. "We needed a fourth wheel and we're lucky you came along."

Their words had me feeling all fuzzy and warm. "Thanks, you guys," I said. "I think you're the best friends I've ever had." It was true.

"Of course we are," Taylor said with a grin. "We're the best friends any of us have had."

Kim's mom set a tray of mini cupcakes in front of us, each frosted in a bright color.

"Okay, enough with the mushy stuff," Taylor said,

smiling as she grabbed a mint chocolate chip cupcake. "Let's eat!"

But Sasha looked at me before digging in. "Anything else we should know?" she asked.

"Just one last thing," I said.

My friends all looked at me, waiting.

"I really hate mushrooms!" I exclaimed.

And at that everyone burst out laughing.

14

I was stuffed after the Rox, but as soon as I got home I checked my mom's menu on the whiteboard and began chopping up cabbage for dinner. I wanted everything to go smoothly because my friends were right: It was time for me to talk to my mom.

I waited until we were sitting down in front of steaming plates of moo shu pork that had magically restored my appetite. My mom was frowning and for a second my resolve wavered. But then I saw my mom glance toward Lily's usual spot and the thought of my beloved dog and the shelter gave me the courage I needed.

"Mom, I have to talk to you about something," I said, setting down my chopsticks.

My mom raised her eyebrows. "I hope it's not about that dog," she said.

The familiar burn of anger started in my belly, but I took a deep breath before answering. "It is, actually, and about the shelter, too," I said calmly.

My mom scowled and then took a bite of her meal.

"Sometimes the way you talk about Lily and the shelter hurts my feelings," I said.

My mom looked puzzled and I realized what my friends had said was true. My mom really didn't know that she'd upset me. "What do you mean?" she asked. "How do I hurt your feelings?"

"When you call Lily 'that dog,'" I said. "And the way you talk about the shelter like it's this terrible place."

My mom opened her mouth but I pushed on,

knowing I needed to say it all and say it now, before I lost my nerve again. "I love the shelter," I said. "It's special to me. It's like a second home, a place where I can just be myself, and my friends there are the best friends I've ever had."

My mom sat back, looking surprised again. "I hadn't realized that," she said.

"I was really lonely when we first moved here," I admitted, playing with one of my chopsticks. "Joining the Dog Club changed that."

"Sweetie, I didn't know you were having trouble making friends," my mom said, concerned.

"I probably should have told you," I said. "But I felt kind of embarrassed about it."

My mom gave a small smile. "Making friends is hard," she said. "I haven't had much luck with it since we moved here either."

And now I was the one who was surprised. Though as I thought about it I realized I shouldn't have been. Back in DC my mom had gone out to movies with a crowd of neighbors, had a monthly book group, and was always meeting friends for coffee. But here she just worked. I'd assumed that was because starting a business was a challenge, but clearly it was more than that.

"I'm glad you told me," I said.

My mom reached over and patted my hand. "Me too," she said. "I think it's made me a bit short tempered. Perhaps that's why I've been somewhat callous about your Dog Club."

That made a lot of sense.

"If the shelter is this important to you, I'll be more respectful when I talk about it," she continued. "And about that—I mean, about *Lily*, too."

I smiled. "Thanks," I said. "That means a lot to me."

I noticed my mom look toward Lily's spot again.

"You know, I think you miss Lily, too," I said hopefully. Missing Lily felt like a permanent ache in my heart.

"Miss that spreader of dog hair?" my mom asked

sharply, then clapped a hand over her mouth. "Whoops," she said. "This is going to take me some time to get used to."

"You know, one of my problems when we first moved here was that I said stuff before I thought about it," I said. "And sometimes what I said was pretty mean."

My mom's eyes stayed on me as she took a bite of pork. She really was trying to listen to me.

"So I've been working on that, taking a deep breath before I respond to things that make me angry," I said. "Maybe you could do that too."

My mom nodded. "I think that's excellent advice." She smiled at me warmly. "Where did you get such wisdom, Bun?"

I grinned as I scooped up a big bite. "I inherited it from my mom."

15

I was happy to have started working things out with my mom, but I still felt empty the next day when I woke up with no Lily. That was going to take a while to get used to. Or maybe I would always miss her just a little.

"How did it go?" Kim asked when I'd reached the corner where we met up before school. Sasha and Taylor were already there, listening eagerly.

"It was really good," I said. There was a brisk breeze

and we began walking toward school. "You guys were right. My mom really didn't know that she was making me feel bad. She's going to try to think before she says stuff, just like me."

"Awesome," Taylor said happily.

"Good for you for talking to her," Kim said, smiling at me as the wind whipped her short hair against her cheeks.

"Yeah, that can be hard," Sasha said. "But worth it."

I thought of the new understanding I had of my mom, who was lonely just like I had been. And who was going to try to change the way she spoke to me because she loved me. "Yeah, totally worth it," I agreed.

We stopped at the light and waited to cross.

"Bri, I love that bun," Sasha said.

I'd done the sock bun again and fastened it with a bright pink band that matched my shirt. "Thanks," I said. "I can show you how to do it if you want."

"That would be awesome," Sasha said happily.

"Maybe you can give me some hair advice, too," Kim said as the light changed and we crossed. "I'm thinking of letting it grow, but I can never figure out how to style it and it just hangs in my eyes all day."

"I'd love to," I said, already considering what might work best with Kim's soft, fine hair.

"See how much we need you, fourth wheel?" Taylor asked, grinning.

I grinned back. I might have lost Lily, but I had my mom and I had my friends. And that was pretty awesome!

Lily galloped over to me as soon as I walked into the shelter that afternoon. She nearly trampled Coco and Waffles in her rush to greet me.

"I miss you too," I told her, freeing the other dogs from their leashes so I could hug Lily.

She climbed right into my lap and wouldn't stop licking my face until I squealed with laughter.

"Looks like someone's happy to see you," Alice said.

She was holding a clipboard in one hand and petting Boxer with the other.

"Yeah, it's mutual," I said, wrapping my arms around Lily and wishing I never had to let her go.

But then Sasha came in with Gus, Jinx, and Hattie, and Lily jumped off me to greet them. Moments later Taylor, Mr. S, Popsicle, and Humphrey came in, followed by Kim and Missy.

"The gang's all here," Alice said cheerfully as the dogs were released from their leashes and began romping about the room. Tim threw a tennis ball that Lily, Daisy, Gus, Mr. S, Tuesday, and Waffles chased while Caley accepted Boxer's Frisbee and sent it whizzing across the room. Caley probably had the strongest throwing arm of all of us and the Frisbee bounced off the wall, much to Boxer's delight.

"I want to make sure we're set for the festival on Saturday," Alice said as Oscar jumped down from his perch and twined around her ankles, delicately stepping around Missy and Humphrey, who were at Alice's feet.

"Good idea," Kim said from where she had sat down to snuggle Gracie. "The Lopezes are bringing the candy to the booth in the morning."

"I can't wait to see how it looks," Caley said.

"Who cares how it looks?" Tim teased. "I can't wait to taste it."

I giggled at that.

"My mom is picking up the bags and calendars on Friday," Sasha said from the corner where she was playing tug-of-war with Jinx. "She and Taylor's dad will drop them off at the booth before the festival starts."

"That reminds me," Alice said, absently removing a strand of dog hair from her T-shirt that had a colorful parade of dogs marching across the front. "The festival starts at ten, so I think we should all be there by nine thirty. Does that sound okay?"

"That's early for a weekend," Tim said.

Caley rolled her eyes. "But worth it for a good cause," she pointed out. "Though if you want to come late you'll just be stuck standing at the booth since there won't be enough stools for all of us."

"Are you saying you wouldn't give up your stool for me?" Tim asked in mock dismay.

Caley laughed. "That's exactly what I'm saying."

"Then I guess I'll be there at nine thirty," Tim said with a loud sigh.

"And I'll bring Tuesday for the first dog shift at the booth after I swing by the shelter to give the dogs breakfast," Alice said.

That reminded me that the second dog at the booth would be Lily. I knew it would be wonderful if we found a family to adopt her, but the thought of her leaving made my chest ache.

"Everyone should wear their Roxbury Park Dog Club T-shirts," Sasha reminded us.

"And my mom said she'll bring a box of sandwiches and drinks from the Rox over to us for lunch," Kim said.

"Yum," Caley said.

"That's so nice of her," Alice added.

"She wanted to do something to help," Kim said, and I heard a note of pride in her voice. Not that I blamed her. Things were better with my mom, but we were still a long way from her supporting the club and what we did here, the way the other parents did.

"Okay, I think we're set," Alice said, heading back to her office.

"That means it's time for doggy basketball," Tim announced, tugging the laundry basket off the toy shelf. "Bri, you get first pick."

Soon we had dogs and people divided into teams. Caley, as ref, threw out the ball, and Lily, who was on my team of course, leaped up and grabbed it.

"Go, Lily!" I shouted, pumping a fist in the air as Lily made a wild run for the basket, Boxer, Daisy, Mr. S, Jinx, and Tuesday hot on her heels. Hattie ran past with a tennis ball and Tim was running after her shouting, "Wrong ball!"

Lily turned and skidded a bit on the floor, her nails scraping as Sasha, my assistant coach, cheered her on.

Missy, who was usually calm, ran in to join the fray, and Popsicle confused everyone by dashing past with an orange ball that looked just like the one we were using for the game.

"Put it in the basket!" Tim called to Popsicle as he tripped over Boxer and fell to the floor, uninjured and laughing.

"That's cheating!" I yelled, because Popsicle wasn't on my team. I charged after Popsicle as the big group of dogs came flying by. There was barking, laughing, dog nails scraping, and of course, the sound of us cheering the dogs on. In other words, complete chaos.

And that was when I looked over and saw someone standing by the front door of the shelter, watching us. Someone who looked a lot like my mother.

"Mom?" I gasped, stopping in my tracks. Tuesday nearly crashed into me but ducked past at the last second.

"Hi, Bri," my mom said. I couldn't read her expression as she watched the ruckus taking over the shelter.

"Score!" Tim shouted as Hattie dunked the ball, and my mom winced slightly.

"Um, guys, this is my mom," I said, then shouted since no one could hear.

Everyone trooped over to say hi to my mom.

"Your stir-fried beef is the best I've ever had," Taylor told my mom after I'd introduced her.

"We all steal Bri's leftovers at lunch," Sasha added, and Kim grinned sheepishly.

My mom smiled. "You'll have to come over for dinner sometime so you can have it fresh."

"Sounds good," Taylor said. "Thanks."

Just then Lily, who had been busy wrestling the ball from Jinx, realized who was here. She raced over and threw herself at my mom's feet, panting happily.

I held my breath, worried my mom would say something about Lily's fur or the way she was drooling a bit on my mom's black boots. But my mom surprised me by squatting down so she could give Lily a good belly rub.

By now Alice had come out of her office, and once my mom stood up I introduced them. I couldn't help wondering what my mom, in her neat khaki pants and fitted blouse, would think of Alice's work clothes: a baggy T-shirt, old jeans, and beat-up sneakers. Though of course my mom just smiled politely as she shook Alice's hand.

"It's so nice to meet another person crazy enough to work full-time with dogs," Alice said warmly, and my mom laughed.

"It does take a certain breed," my mom said.

Alice cracked up at the joke and my mom grinned again, a real grin. Lily stood up and leaned against my mom's legs so my mom could pet her head.

"I'm glad you came to visit," Alice said. "Make yourself at home and let me know if I can answer any questions. Though of course, Bri knows everything." She shot me a smile. "We're so pleased she's come on board."

My mom glanced around at the chaos but then

smiled. "She's pretty happy about it and I can see why. It's like a party in here."

Alice laughed. "That's one word for it," she said comfortably. "I suspect you're a bit more organized at the Pampered Puppy."

My mom bit her lip for a moment. "We are, but I'm starting to learn that there's more than one way to care for dogs."

I beamed at that.

Alice smiled too. "Maybe we can get coffee sometime and trade stories," she said.

My mom's eyes lit up at this and I felt a rush of gratitude to Alice for reaching out to my mom. I never could have imagined it before today, but maybe Alice would be my mom's first friend in Roxbury Park.

"I'd like that," my mom said. "And there is actually something you can help me with today." She looked down at Lily, whose head was pressed against her leg. Then her eyes found me. "Bri, you were right. I did miss Lily, a lot. I think that's why I snapped at you—I was missing her but wasn't ready to admit it yet. And now I've come around. Lily's sweet and loving and everything we could ever want in a dog."

I held my breath, not daring to hope that she was saying what I thought she might be saying.

"So how about you and me fill out adoption papers so we can take Lily home with us, where she belongs?" my mom asked.

For a second I couldn't believe I had heard right. But then Taylor, Kim, and Sasha shrieked and threw their arms around me, Caley cheered, and Tim let out a loud whoop.

My mom looked at me inside the tangle of my friends and grinned. "I'll take that as a yes," she said.

16

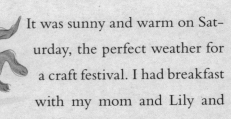

It was sunny and warm on Saturday, the perfect weather for a craft festival. I had breakfast with my mom and Lily and then headed into town. There were booths all along Main Street, which was closed to traffic for the day. Stores had tables out front and the doors to the community center were open so that everyone could see the art display inside. There was a clown juggling and a band setting up in front of town hall. It was like walking through the best and biggest birthday party ever, and it hadn't even officially started yet!

"Hey, Bri," Alice said when I arrived at the booth. All the booths were a simple white, and ours had a sign that proclaimed "Roxbury Park Shelter and Dog Club" on the front.

I greeted Alice and Tuesday, who was freshly brushed and looked excited to be part of things.

A moment later Kim came up, then Caley and Tim. "Dibs on a stool," Tim called as he came inside the booth. His hair stood up on one side of his head like he'd just rolled out of bed. Which he probably had.

Alice grinned. "There are enough for all of us," she said.

"But I thought there was a big rush to get a seat," Tim said, looking accusingly at Caley, who raised up her hands.

"I had to get you here on time," Caley said playfully.

"Okay, but you owe me a cup of coffee," Tim

grumbled, though I could see him hiding a smile.

"Fair enough," Caley said. "Alice, do you want some too? I'll make a run."

But before Alice could answer, Sasha and her mom and Taylor and her dad arrived, each carrying a big cardboard box.

"Oh, I can't wait to see how our bags turned out!" Kim cried.

"And the calendars," Taylor added, setting down one of the cartons.

We opened the top box, which turned out to be the calendars, and paged through. The paper was thick and glossy and the photos were so good it looked professional.

"These are awesome," Tim proclaimed, and everyone else agreed.

"Okay, let's see the bags," I said eagerly.

Sasha's mom opened the carton and Alice passed them out to each of us. The bags were made out of a sturdy canvas and I nearly gasped when I saw how cool the silhouette looked.

"These are going to go like hotcakes," Alice predicted.

"Yeah, they are fantastic," Sasha's mom agreed. "I hope you're proud, Bri. The logo looks like it was created by a pro."

I beamed as everyone else chimed in about how good they looked.

"I have a great idea," Kim said, her eyes lighting up as she looked from me to the bag. "Bri, you should be in charge of our website, the art part."

"That would be awesome," Taylor agreed. "You can make it look all cool with a new layout every week. And add in the logo and this picture and any other designs you come up with."

"It would raise our profile if our website was dynamic like that," Sasha said, in full businesswoman mode. She glanced at her mom, who nodded.

"I'd love to," I said. And I realized that this was the last barrier: now I wasn't just a member of the Dog

Club—I had a role that was all mine. And a role I knew I'd love.

We began setting up our booth, arranging the bags and calendars, plus a big pile of flyers about the fostering program and a clipboard where people could sign up to begin the foster process. Alice also set out a box for donations. And a few minutes later the Lopezes arrived with the candy.

"I think it turned out great," Carmen said as she helped us pile it up on platters, the foil glittery in the sun. "And they taste pretty good, too, if I do say so myself."

"I can help you judge that," Tim said, reaching for one.

"Why don't we each take just one," Alice said, sounding like a preschool teacher. "We want these to help get the word out about the fostering program."

"And to raise money for the Dog Club and shelter," Caley reminded Tim.

"Got it," he said, already unwrapping his.

We each took one and just as Carmen said, they were delish, the caramel silky and sweet and the chocolate smooth and rich.

Main Street was starting to fill with people: the festival had begun.

"Hey, everyone," Mrs. Washington said, waving as she and Gus walked by.

A moment later a woman stopped at the booth. "So you guys run a foster program?" she asked. "I think this would be perfect for my mom. She loves dogs but travels to Florida every winter so she can't own one."

"Let me tell you about what we're doing," Alice said, passing the woman a flyer and explaining the program.

"Can I have some candy?" a little boy asked, his dad coming up behind.

"This is for people helping dogs find homes, Johnny," the dad said. "Not a candy booth."

"I'm scared of dogs," Johnny said.

But just then he caught sight of sweet little Tuesday

with her big eyes and soft fur. "But this one seems okay," Johnny said slowly.

"Do you want to pet her?" Kim asked, looking over at Johnny's dad to make sure it was okay.

"I think so," Johnny said, looking both scared and brave as his dad nodded encouragingly. "Yes."

Kim walked Johnny over and Tuesday sniffed his hand, then gave him a kiss on the cheek. Johnny blinked and then smiled. "I like this dog," he said happily. "Does she need a home?"

"She does," Kim said. "And if it's okay with your dad, you can have one of our dog paw candies."

But Johnny was too excited about Tuesday to care about candy. He was petting her while Tuesday leaned against him.

"Wow, Johnny, Mom is going to be so happy to hear there's a dog you like," the dad said. He looked at us. "And surprised. We've wanted to get a dog for a while, but with Johnny's fears we couldn't."

"It looks like he and Tuesday are getting along

pretty well," Taylor said hopefully. Johnny was now sitting down and pulling an agreeable Tuesday into his lap.

"I'm texting Mom," Johnny's dad told him, pulling out his phone. "We need her to come over so we can see about taking this dog home."

Johnny cheered while Taylor, Sasha, Kim, and I exchanged gleeful looks. The festival was off to a great start!

By late afternoon we'd handed out all our flyers and Alice had needed to run back to the shelter to print out more. All our bags were sold, as well as the calendars and candy, and our donations box was full. Best of all, Tuesday was going to be adopted and there was a stack of applications from people interested in fostering dogs.

"I think it's about time to pack up," Alice said.

But just then I caught sight of two familiar figures. "Hi, Mom," I called as she came up with Lily, a box from Bundt Cake Bakery in her arms.

Lily happily greeted me and I bent down to hug her. I still couldn't believe she was mine.

"I thought you guys might want a snack," my mom said, setting down the box and opening it up to reveal a dozen cinnamon doughnut twists.

"We do," Tim said happily, grabbing for one.

"Thanks, Mom," I said, feeling proud as everyone took the treat my mom had brought. Now she was one of the parents supporting us!

"Tell me about the day," she said to us all. "I hope you got a lot of people willing to foster." She grinned and caught my eye. "Because you never know when someone might just fall in love with a foster dog."

"The Roxbury Park Dog Club strikes again," Taylor said happily.

My mom laughed. "Your club really *is* pretty special," she said.

My heart was full as I looked down at sweet Lily, who was now mine, and at my friends, who were so happy for me they were beaming.

And then I threw my arms around my mom, who finally understood how much it all meant to me.

The Roxbury Park Dog Club really had struck again—and it had made me the happiest girl in the world!

DON'T MISS THE NEXT

DOG CLUB ADVENTURE!

Sasha feels like she does more work for the Club than any of the other girls—and the stress is starting to affect their friendship. Can the Dog Club survive its first big fight?

1

The halls of Roxbury Park Middle School were packed with kids talking and laughing as I wove my way toward my best friend Kim's locker. That was our official meeting place after the last bell rang every day and today I was running a little late.

"Hi, Sasha," Kim said when I finally made it.

"Let's get going," my other best friend, Taylor, said with an easy grin as she slung her bag over her shoulder.

It was so bulky and heavy it took her two tries. "I don't want to be late for class." Taylor, who was the newer of my best friends, took fabulous pictures and had just started studying advanced photography at the Roxbury Park Art Center.

"And I'm helping my mom out at the Pampered Puppy today, so I should hustle too," Bri said.

Bri was the newest member of our pack and in some ways I was still getting to know her. She was also the newest member of the Roxbury Park Dog Club, which Kim, Taylor, and I had founded at the start of the year. Seventh graders at Roxbury Park Middle School were required to do community service and the three of us had signed up to work at the local dog shelter, an amazing place that took in homeless dogs and kept them safe and happy until they found new homes. But Alice, who ran the shelter, was having trouble making ends meet. At the same time, Kim's neighbors were looking for someone to walk their dog, Humphrey, in the afternoons before they got home from work. In a flash of brilliance Kim realized that if we started a dog club after school at the shelter, dogs could get a few hours of much needed exercise and fun, and we could bring in some extra money for the shelter. Many of the dogs' owners also signed up for pickup service, which meant we'd swing by their homes on the way to club meetings and walk the dogs to the shelter. It cost a bit extra but was worth it for owners who were busy at work.

"Did you guys get that email from Alice last night?" Kim asked. "The one with a picture of Coco in her new home?" The big black and brown dog had been one of our earliest club members and I was sad to see her go, but the picture last night had definitely showed us all how happy she was.

"She's living the doggy dream," Taylor said, making us laugh. Coco's owner had moved to a big farm in Pennsylvania, with acres of land to run on and lots of ducks and squirrels to chase. It really was the doggy dream and I was happy Coco got to live it.

"We have to figure out how many new dogs we can

take into the club now that Coco's gone," Kim said as the four of us walked toward the door.

The club had been a huge success, especially after we'd been featured in the local newspaper with pictures taken by Taylor. Now we had a wait list and Alice had been able to start up a new venture, a foster program for dogs. We were all huge fans of that project, but it definitely kept Alice busy.

"How many club dogs are there now?" Taylor asked as we walked down the front path of the school. Kids milled around us and a football whizzed past between a pair of eighth graders.

"Popsicle, Jinx, Waffles, Missy, Hattie, and Humphrey," Bri said as she ticked off on her fingers. Sometimes it still surprised me that Bri was a club member. Not so long ago she'd been mean to Taylor, jealous that Taylor had been the new girl but fit in so seamlessly. To make matters worse, Bri's mom, who owned a fancy doggy day care, had tried to take our club down. For a while their aggressive advertising plan had worked, but in the end we all realized that there was room in town for two dog care centers. At the same time Bri realized that Taylor was awesome while Taylor, with her big heart, realized Bri just needed friends. Bri began hanging out at the shelter and loved it so much that we asked her to join the club. "Plus Daisy and Gus—and of course Mr. S and Lily." She shot me a grin when she said the last two names and I grinned right back. Bri and I had both adopted shelter dogs, and they loved going back to visit their pals.

My parents got divorced when I was little, so it was just me and my mom, which could get a little lonely. Bringing Mr. S home had totally fixed that, and I adored my snuggly Cavachon with all my heart. Lately he'd been taking up a lot more of my time though. Mr. S was an older dog and as a result needed to go out more often. Of course I always took him—I needed my sweet pup comfortable, and my mom, who was a bit of a neat freak, did not want an accident in the house. But with everything else I had going on, the extra walks were tough.

"That's ten club dogs," Kim said. The brisk wind whipping the fall leaves off the trees had turned her cheeks pink. Winter was not far off and I was glad I'd worn my thick green fleece. I didn't want my muscles to get cold on the walk over to dance rehearsal. My mom used to drive me, but she was extra busy at work right now and it really wasn't a long walk to the studio.

"I think we could take in two more dogs since there are four of us plus Tim and Caley," Kim continued. Tim and Caley were high schoolers who volunteered at the shelter with us. At first it had been a little intimidating to work with older kids, but now we were all really comfortable together. "And that would bring our total to twelve club dogs."

"That sounds good," Taylor said, smoothing down her braids. Despite her efforts, the beads at the ends were clinking musically in the wind.

"So you'll call the next people on the wait list?" Bri said to me in her direct way. Even though she worked hard to control her temper, there were still times when she was blunt in a way that could sting. I knew this wasn't one of those times: handling new clients was part of my job at the club, so of course she'd ask me about it. But it still made my stomach tighten up because I really did not have time to call anyone, let alone a family from the wait list who would have a ton of questions and take ages to schedule for their trial visit.

"I'll try to get to it tonight if I have time," I said, absently twisting a curl around my fingers. Bri and I were both wearing our long hair in ponytails but mine was sloppy, with curls leaking out, while Bri's straight black hair was sleek, with a few carefully curled strands framing her face. She was twisting the jade charm she always wore on a red string around her neck—Bri was Chinese American and she had told us that the pendant was for good luck.

"We're all going to be pretty pressed for time with that report we have to do for social studies," Kim said with a sigh as we waited for a car to pass before crossing Market Street. Kim struggled in school and recently her parents had considered sending her to private school. Eventually they'd agreed to let her stay with us at Roxbury Park Middle School but it was on the condition that she keep her grades up. Tutoring sessions with Taylor's math genius older sister, Anna, helped a lot, but Kim still got anxious, especially when we had big assignments. And the cultural essays that Mr. Martin had announced today were definitely intimidating. That was a big reason I was so stressed, too—I had no extra time, so how was I supposed to write ten pages about Mongolia, a country I knew nothing about?

"I wish he'd let us choose the place we were studying," Taylor said. "I'd rather learn about Egypt or France than Iceland."

"I think Iceland is partly covered by glaciers," Bri said. She'd lucked out with Italy. She could write about yummy food and the painting on the ceiling of the Sistine Chapel, and she'd be done in no time, unlike the rest of us. "That could be cool to write about."

"I need to find something interesting like that about

Tanzania," Kim said. Her cheeks were now pale, a sure sign she was feeling anxious.

"I think they have lions there," I said, remembering something my mom had said about endangered species. She had started an environmental law firm where Taylor's dad worked too and she liked talking about her cases. "You could write about that."

"Lions are definitely cool," she said thoughtfully. "Okay, maybe this report won't be so bad."

If only there were lions in Mongolia.

"Yeah, I don't think it will be that big a deal," Bri agreed. "And Sasha, I don't think calling families on the wait list will take that long. We don't want people waiting forever and not hearing from us."

I felt a slight flash of irritation at her pushiness. That was total Bri, of course, and I liked it when she was pushing to help the dogs or telling an eighth grader to give us space in the hall. But it wasn't so great when it felt like she was nagging me.

"We know you're busy practicing for your

performance though," Kim said, smiling at me and cheering me right up. Dogs and dance were my two favorite things and when I wasn't at our club, I was at the dance studio, where I took three classes a week as a member of the junior company. Our first big recital was coming up in a few weeks, so I was extra busy with rehearsals, especially since I had a solo in our jazz number.

"We'll be in the front row," Taylor promised. "I can't wait to see you do your thing."

It was funny to think that Taylor had only moved here from North Carolina this summer since it felt like I'd known her forever. Kim had been coming to my shows for years and always brought me a bouquet of pink roses, my favorite. But this would be the first time Taylor and Bri would be there and I was excited. And a little nervous—I had a lot of work to do if I wanted to be ready. "I'm glad you guys will be there," I said. "But it *is* going to keep me pretty busy."

"Yeah, that makes sense. I can't wait to see you

perform either," Bri said immediately, the warmth in her voice wiping away the last traces of the annoyance I had felt.

"Do you get to wear a really cool costume?" she went on.

And her words made me realize something that froze me in my tracks, like my shoes were suddenly glued to the ground.

"What's wrong?" Kim asked, seeing the expression on my face.

"I forgot my dance bag at school," I gasped. I could picture exactly where it was, on the hook at the back of my locker. I'd planned to grab it last, but then I'd gotten distracted debating whether I needed to bring home my science binder and now, instead of hanging from my shoulder, it was still dangling in my empty locker.

"Can you dance without your stuff?" Taylor asked, her brown eyes full of concern.

"No," I said, taking a deep breath. "I have to go back for it. I'll see you guys later."

My friends called good-bye as I took off running back toward school. But I knew no matter how fast I went I was going to be late for class and Madame Florence, my dance teacher, was not going to be pleased at all.

It was not a good start to the afternoon!

JOIN THE

Roxbury Park ♦ D🐶g Club

With great friends and plenty of cuddly canines,
this series is **impawsible** to put down!

HARPER
An Imprint of HarperCollinsPublishers

www.harpercollinschildrens.com